The Dream Watcher

The Dream Watcher

BARBARA WERSBA

Front Street
Asheville, North Carolina

I gratefully acknowledge the permission to reprint
the following extracts:

Wilfred Owen, four lines from "Anthem for Doomed Youth"
from THE COLLECTED POEMS OF WILFRED OWEN,
Copyright © Chatto and Windus Ltd. 1946, 1963.
Reprinted by permission of New Directions Publishing Company,
Mr. Harold Owen, and Chatto & Windus Ltd.

George Bernard Shaw, from "Heartbreak House": FOUR PLAYS BY
BERNARD SHAW. Copyright © 1953 by Random House, Inc.
Reprinted by permission of the Society of Authors, London.

Reprinted from LETTERS TO A YOUNG POET by Rainer Maria Rilke.
Translation by M. D. Herter Norton. By permission of
W. W. Norton & Company, Inc. and Insel Verlag, Wiesbaden,
West Germany. Copyright © 1934 by W. W. Norton &
Company, Inc. Copyright renewed 1962 by M. D. Herter Norton.
Revised Edition copyright 1954 by W. W. Norton & Company, Inc.

Copyright © 1968 by Barbara Wersba
All rights reserved
Originally published by Atheneum, 1968
Printed in the United States
First Front Street paperback edition, 2004
Designed by Helen Robinson

Library of Congress Cataloging-in-Publication Data
Wersba, Barbara
The dream watcher. [1st ed.] New York, Atheneum, 1968.
p. cm.
Summary: A teenager considers himself the
"All-American" failure until he meets an eccentric old lady who
helps him to see the true value of being an individual.
ISBN 1-932425-08-X
[1. YouthFiction.]
PZ7.W473 Dr
[Fic]   68028750

The Dream Watcher

1 I'd better begin this story by telling you that until a month ago I was quite a mess. I mean, I was such a mess that my mother wanted to send me to a psychiatrist but backed down when she discovered that it would cost twenty-five dollars an hour. Twenty-five dollars an hour was too much even for her. It wouldn't have done any good anyway, the psychiatrist, because whatever is wrong with me is not in my head. It's in my soul. That's a square word, I know, but it's what I mean. Not that I'm religious or anything. When I say soul, I mean the part of a person that is his best part. The part that made Shakespeare write the way he did, and the part that made Einstein such a good man. Not just good as a scientist, but as a person, too. To me, the soul is the most exciting thing there is. But most people have crummy souls, and before I met Mrs. Woodfin mine was in pretty bad shape.

This story is more about Mrs. Woodfin than anyone else, but in order to get to her I have to describe a lot of other things. Mrs. Woodfin won't mean much to you unless you understand what a mess I was, and what my parents are like, and how we live.

Take my mother. Her idea of life is to move to Beverly Hills, California, and have a swimming pool and servants and TV in every room. She would also like to have a Cadillac and a mink coat and a husband who was a movie producer or something. But the truth of the matter is that we live in a housing development in New Jersey and drive a Ford and are always in debt. That's what bugs my mother. Most of the time she is either reading fashion magazines or watching old Bette Davis movies on television, and whereas you would think these things would make her happy because she does them so much, they don't make her happy. They make her irritable. Even the TV commercials make her irritable, because they are always telling you to buy a bigger and better thing than the one you have just bought. And she believes them.

Not that we are candidates for the Poverty Program. Our house, which is in this development called Blythewoode, has a big TV antenna that rotates, and a washer-drier, and two air conditioners, and an oven that cleans itself. The trouble is, these things are always breaking down. Which brings me to the subject of my father.

A couple of years ago I saw this great play on television—*Death Of A Salesman*. If you saw it too, then you saw my father, because he is just like the hero in it. The trouble is, the man wasn't a hero at all and neither is my father. My father, whose name is John Scully, is an insurance salesman. He sits in this big office in New York City with fifty other people and tries to sell insurance. Judging from the business he does, I would say that people aren't insuring things much anymore. I mean, he doesn't make very much money and is always over his head in installment payments. No sooner does he buy my mother one thing than it collapses and he has to begin a set of payments on a better model. That's how he is like the man in the play, Willy Loman. You see, Willy Loman once had dreams of a better life and so did my father. Before he met my mother he had done some flying and wanted to be an airline pilot. But then he met her and she had a cousin in this insurance business who said he could set my father up. So he took the job thinking he would get promoted to the executive level. Well, he never got promoted and is still selling insurance. But sometimes in the summer when we are all sitting in the back yard, a jet will roar by on its way to Newark Airport and my father will look up at it with this funny expression on his face. I never ask him what he is thinking at these moments, because I know.

Just one more thing about *Death of A Salesman*. There is a line in it where the salesman's wife says, "He's a human being, and a terrible thing is happening to him. So attention must be paid."

That's the way I feel about my father.

Now that I've told you about my parents, I'd better get back to myself, which is the hardest part of the story because it's depressing. You see, it wasn't just that I was lousy in school. Or that I didn't have friends or belong to any clubs or like to dance. It wasn't even that I was funny-looking. A lot of kids in my class are funny-looking and are quite popular. In fact there is one guy in my class who looks like an ape but is terribly popular because he smokes marijuana. Which seems a stupid reason to be popular, but he is. No, the problem with me was my soul. This may sound weird, but sometimes I felt like my soul was a trapped animal banging wildly around a cage trying to get out. A rhinoceros maybe. I could almost feel it crashing around in my body, banging its head on the bars. It really made me nervous. Here I was, Albert Scully, a very ordinary person with soul-trouble. It was almost laughable. Mrs. Woodfin could have explained the whole thing to me in about ten seconds, but I hadn't met her then. All I knew was that I was in trouble.

Not that there's anything unusual about being in trouble. In my school the more trouble you are in, the more fascinating you are. But trouble to the other kids is getting caught driving without a license or showing up drunk at a dance or cheating on exams. Whereas my trouble was simply being a total failure. Looking back on it, I could see that I had been a failure from around the age of four when I couldn't even handle crayons in nursery school. One week in nursery school, and I was already an underachiever. And ever since then people had been telling me to get with it. My mother wanted me to get with it, and my relatives wanted me to get with it, and my teachers wanted me to get with it. And I couldn't get with anything.

It's like this. No matter how anybody else in the entire world reacted to a thing, I would react differently. For example, my uncle would come to the house for dinner and get going on the Vietnam war, saying how it was such a just cause and how it would stop the spread of Communism. Whereas all I could think of was those poor little oriental people getting hurt and burned and having their farms blown up. It may be terrible to say this, but I didn't care whether Communism was spreading or not.

Or for another example, there was this teacher in my school called Mr. Thompson, who taught History and was a mess. He had bad breath and dandruff and wore suits from the 1940's or something. The other kids thought he was an idiot, and one day this kid I told you about, the one who smokes marijuana, wrote a four-letter word on the blackboard before Thompson came in and the poor guy was so embarrassed he didn't even ask who had done it. Any other teacher would have asked who had done it, but poor Thompson just erased it with his dandruff falling all over the place and his trousers sagging. The point is, I liked Thompson better than any teacher in the school.

No matter what I liked, it was peculiar. That's what worried me. I liked taking long walks and Shakespeare and collecting recipes, and going to the Natural History Museum, and sometimes just riding on the Fifth Avenue bus in New York. I even liked gardening. Which embarrassed my mother but I really liked it. I mean, I planted a tree in our back yard that actually grew. It's the only tree there and is very healthy.

If this isn't too boring, I'll tell you a few more things that I liked. I liked Channel 13 on television because it showed foreign plays, and I liked the *National Geographic* magazine because it sometimes had articles on New Zealand. New Zealand is about my favorite country in the world because it seems so beautiful and unspoiled and has no air pollution. I also liked going to the local library on Saturday. And that's what killed my mother. Here was all my homework undone, and there I was going off to the library to read novels. Not that other kids don't read novels. They do. But what they read are James Jones and Harold Robbins and John O'Hara, and almost anything that is dirty but which seems like literature. To be perfectly frank with you, other people's sex lives don't turn me on. What's the point of reading about everyone else making out when you don't have the courage to make out yourself? That's one of the main criticisms I have of the guys in my school. They are always pretending that they've had these fantastic sex experiences when all they know about it is from books. As a matter of fact, I think their attitude towards sex is depressing. Because I am almost totally convinced that the point of sex is not to get some poor girl in the back of some broken-down car and make her hysterical. I don't think girls even like wrestling around in somebody's father's car and losing their reason. I don't know. I'm probably neurotic or impotent or something, but I don't think sex should be crude.

The reason I brought up the library a few seconds ago is because it was just one more thing about me that was peculiar. Because I would take out ten or twelve books at a time and actually read them. The authors I liked best were Thomas Wolfe and Thoreau and Edgar Lee Masters and Walt Whitman and Saroyan. At one point I had tried to read Hemingway and Fitzgerald and all that crowd because my father had read them once, but I didn't dig them. I realize that Hemingway is supposed to be a very great American writer, but he makes me suspicious because he is always describing bullfights and safaris and making himself out to be so masculine that any guy who reads him is bound to feel inferior.

I also liked an author called Sherwood Anderson and one that my father had never heard of called James Agee. The thing that was depressing was that none of these authors were on my school reading list. Which meant that I had no one to discuss them with. But every time I found something I liked in a book, I would type it out and paste it on the wall over my desk. There must have been a thousand quotations pasted up there and it made me feel good just to glance up and see some great thought that a man had had years before. One quotation that I particularly liked was from Thoreau, who was a person who lived alone in the woods for a long time because he loved Nature so much. He really did. Wild birds and animals would make friends with him and everything, and so he just lived in this place called Walden Pond even though everyone else thought he was off his rocker. Anyway, this was the quotation:

I went to the woods because I wished to live deliberately, to front only the essential facts of life, and see if I could not learn what it had to teach, and not, when I came to die, discover that I had not lived.

That, in a nutshell, was why my soul was in such bad shape. I hadn't lived anything. And it was absolutely certain that I was going to die someday. That's why I liked this person Thoreau. He made sense.

12

2 I've told you that this story is about Mrs. Woodfin, and it is, except that I haven't gotten to her yet. If I could write like Saroyan or somebody, I would have gotten to her on the first page. But to tell you the truth, I'm a very slow person. If I have to write an essay for school, it takes me about a year because the possibilities seem so vast. Even a stupid topic like "How I Spent My Summer Vacation." This is a quality that drives my mother crazy, but I can't help it. I'm slow.

Anyway, the day I met Mrs. Woodfin was such a terrible day that by the time I did meet her, I was almost insane. Maybe that's why she liked me. Insanity attracts some people. To begin with, I woke up to hear my parents arguing in their room, which is nothing unusual except that it was 6:00 a.m. This morning I was the topic, and so of course I listened.

"I just can't stand it," my mother was saying. "If he were retarded, there might be an excuse, but his I.Q. is perfectly normal. The Principal said so. What's the matter with him?"

"Nothing," said my father. "There's nothing the matter with him."

"Then will you tell me why he is failing every subject? Bob Greenwald's boy is shy too, but he gets A's and is president of the class."

"He is not Bob Greenwald's boy."

"That's the trouble! If he had a father he could respect, he wouldn't have turned out this way. How is he going to make college?"

"Maybe he doesn't want to go to college," said my father.

"Are you out of your mind? *Everybody* goes to college."

"I didn't."

"Ha!" said my mother. "I suppose that's why you're such a big success."

"Helen, please ... I haven't had my coffee yet."

"I want to know what is going to become of that child. I have not worked and sweated and scrimped to have him turn into a dropout."

"What do you want him to be—Secretary of State?"

"Oh, you're funny, John. You're an absolute riot. You spend half the day in some bar in New York and then come home and pass out. He's your only child. Don't you care about him?"

"I don't know if I care about anything," said my father..

Even though there was a wall between us, I could see them in my mind's eye, if there is such a thing. My mother would be wearing a nylon nightgown with her hair in rollers, and she would be pacing the room like Bette Davis, her hips all disjointed. And my father would be sitting on the side of the bed in this ratty old bathrobe he got at Korvette's. He would probably be smoking, even though he says he hates to smoke before breakfast. His hair would be rumpled, and his eyes would have these pouches under them, which my mother says are from drinking but which I think are from misery.

It's funny, because even though they were saying these terrible things about me, I felt more sorry for my father than myself. It was obvious what a failure they thought I was and everything, yet all I could think of was my father and how he went absolutely dead under attack. I'm the same way. If anyone attacks me I get paralyzed. And every time my mother yells at him, he just gets quieter and quieter. I think that's why he drinks.

We're alike in a lot of ways, in the sense that we are both undemonstrative. Once, when I was a very little kid, my mother told me about his wanting to be a pilot, so I went and bought an airplane building set at the dime store and made him this plane. It was a pretty lousy plane, but I worked on it a long time and when I finally gave it to him he didn't say anything. He just stared at it like he was going blind. I mean, he really liked the plane but couldn't show it. That's the trouble. Nobody in our family shows his feelings except my mother, and hers are usually hysterical.

The reason she is always hysterical is obvious to me, though I couldn't explain it to her, and she wouldn't want to know anyway. The reason is this. My mother is a person who walks around being a movie star in her mind. Somebody who sweeps down a marble staircase in a gold dress with a kind of gorgeous yet weary smile on her lips and with some great guy waiting for her at the bottom. Then she comes to and sees that all she has is this five-room house in a development, and me, and my father who is certainly in no way seductive. But it's sad, because she persists in this hang-up even when we're in the A&P. What I mean is, when we go to the A&P my mother is the only person there who is dressed like she was going to Europe. Her hair is all fluffed and sprayed and she has on this very pale makeup which is supposed to be fashionable but which really makes her look ill, and she is wearing high heels. As though there were going to be a Hollywood agent at the check-out counter or something. It used to embarrass me because everyone else's mother looks normal in the A&P. But I've grown used to it.

My parents went on arguing until my mother slammed out of the room, and then there was this depressing silence in the house which made me want to go back to bed. So I did. And Orson jumped in with me and settled down on my stomach. Orson is a cat I've had for around three years, and he is named after Orson Bean, the comedian, because he has such a riotous personality. He really does. For example, this cat Orson will wait for me behind a door all day, and then when I pass it he will jump straight up in the air to frighten me. He frightens me every time, and it's pretty funny.

My mother was having a heart attack about my still being in bed, so I got up and dressed and went into the kitchen. My father was sitting at the table in a dazed sort of way and no one spoke to anyone. The first thing I did was to spill my orange juice on my eggs, and the second thing I did was to read at the table, which my mother hates. The third thing I did was to miss the bus. So by the time I got to school my English class was half over. I seriously considered going home again, but I didn't and walked in anyway and got hell. Mr. Finley, the teacher, was in a wild mood. "Are you some sort of privileged person?" he kept yelling. "Why are you late? Why? Why?" It's odd, but I couldn't remember why. Which is what I told you before. When I'm under attack, I go blank.

The whole day was like that, and by two o'clock I thought I was going insane. I lost my briefcase with all my stuff in it, and then some guy in the locker room accused me of stealing his athletic supporter. As if anyone would steal such a thing. Then my Algebra teacher called me in to say that if I didn't get down to work I would be in high school for the rest of my life. And on top of everything this girl, Sheila Morris, called me a slob. That really hurt because I had once offered to marry her sister.

This is the way it happened. Whereas you are always hearing about teen-age girls getting pregnant, I don't think many of them do, yet one in our school did a year ago. The sister of this girl Sheila Morris. Her name was Doris Morris, which in itself was bad enough, and to make things worse she was highly unattractive. She was a very pathetic girl because she wanted to be liked so much, and I guess this need to be liked was the thing that got her pregnant. The news went like wildfire through the school and the Principal called her in, and this poor girl wouldn't say who had done it. I sort of liked her for that because it showed a sense of honor. I mean, she could easily have said who had done it and ruined the boy's life, but she had a sense of honor. I thought about this for days, and the more I thought about it the more it seemed to me that I should marry her. Not that I liked her. But I realized that no one was ever going to marry Doris Morris, pregnant or not, and that someone should because she had this sense of honor. So I proposed.

My mother had a fit when I told her. "My God," she said, "are you out of your mind? You're only in the eighth grade!" Looking back on it, I can see that my feelings about Doris were rather childish, so it was probably lucky that she turned me down and her parents took her to Utica. But all the same I thought it was a pretty nice gesture, and so I was hurt when her sister called me a slob. I couldn't understand it.

By the time I got home that day, I was in a very foul mood. It was around five o'clock, and my mother was watching an old movie on television that she's already seen a hundred times—*Now Voyager*. It's a terrifically false story about two people—Bette Davis and Paul Henreid—who fall in love on a ship but can't get married because the man is loyal to his mean wife. The reason they fall in love is because Bette Davis has just had psychoanalysis and gotten rid of her inhibitions. They are wildly attracted to each other, but decide that they mustn't ever see each other or make love or anything because of the mean wife. So Bette Davis decides to raise his ugly daughter instead, and you get the impression that this is going to sublimate her passion for the father, who happens to be very good-looking. They meet at the end of the movie for one last time and look out at the stars together, and the whole thing is terrifically false.

Anyway, my mother was watching it as though it were *Hamlet* or something, and when my father came in she didn't notice. My father made himself a double martini and sat down by the window, and I knew immediately that he'd had a bad day. It's like this. If my father comes home and makes a single martini and drinks it slowly, he's had a fairly good day. But if he makes a double and drinks it fast, you can be sure he's depressed. Not that he's a raucous drinker. He just goes to sleep when he's had enough.

Well, he sat there by the window looking out at the development, which is a pretty dull view because all the houses are alike, and there was this look on his face that seemed to say that nothing good was ever going to happen to him again, and that he didn't care if it did. And suddenly I had this wild idea of scooping him up in my arms and soaring into the sky like Superman and carrying him off to some enchanted country where he could be a famous pilot and fly jets a thousand feet long.

This was a great daydream, but it was interrupted by a TV commercial which came on very loud showing the inside of somebody's stomach and what terrible indigestion it was having. You could actually *see* the indigestion, and it was sort of revolting. I hate TV commercials, especially the cigarette ones. They are always showing these gorgeous people smoking their lungs out in country settings with brooks running by—as though smoking were the next best thing to orange juice. If you wanted to believe these commercials, you could die of cancer in about two seconds.

My mother started to file her nails. "Albert, go look at the meat loaf," she said.

"Why should he look at the meat loaf?" asked my father. "The bell rings when it's done."

"The bell is broken," said my mother. "Like everything else."

"Great. What else is broken, if I may inquire?"

"The steam iron and the toastmaster."

"Great," muttered my father. "Marvelous."

I went and looked at the meat loaf. It seemed OK.

"What are your plans for the evening?" said my mother to my father. She sounded very sarcastic. "I mean, how many drinks do you intend to have?"

"Four hundred," said my father.

I thought this was funny, and laughed.

"Be quiet," said my mother. "Do your homework."

I opened my Algebra book but couldn't concentrate very much. My father was staring around the living room like he had never seen it before. The living room is pale green and has furniture from Macy's. First he stared at the Early American cobbler's bench, which we use as a coffee table, and then he stared at the Early American cranberry scoop, which is for holding magazines. Next he stared at the Early American tavern sign over the fireplace, and then he stared at the Boston rocker, which he hates because it's uncomfortable. He and my mother have terrific disputes over furniture because she likes everything to look old even though it's new, whereas he keeps saying that he is not a goddamn Pilgrim Father and doesn't intend to live like one.

The movie came on the screen again. Bette Davis was standing in a train station telling Paul Henreid how she could never see him again, but I didn't believe a word of it.

It was then that we smelled smoke.

"My God. What's burning?" said my mother.

"Probably the house," said my father. He was already a little tight.

"No, it's coming from outside," said my mother. She put her head out the window. "It's the old lady again, burning her garbage. I really cannot stand this anymore. John, will you please ..."

"Oh no," said my father. "Not me. I'm too drunk. I'm an alcoholic."

My mother decided to ignore this. "Albert," she said to me, "I want you to go over to that woman's house and tell her that I will call the police if she burns any more garbage in the yard. It's a health hazard. Furthermore, I want you to tell her that Mr. Gapello picks up garbage three times a week. His number is in the phone book."

"Ah, Mom ..."

"You heard me, Albert."

So I put on my jacket and went. And that was the beginning of the strangest experience of my life.

3 The old lady my mother was talking about lived a few blocks away, and her house was a wreck. It wasn't a development house, because when the real estate people bought the land for the development she wouldn't sell. It made them furious because whereas everything was being torn down to make new houses, she insisted on keeping her old one even though they offered her a fortune for it. So there it sat, looking like something out of Dickens, right in the middle of our development.

I was pretty depressed as I walked over there, because about the last thing in the world I wanted to do was persuade some old lady to stop burning garbage. *I* didn't care if she burned garbage or not, for God's sake. I had had a lousy day and was feeling sad about my father.

I walked along the sidewalk looking at all the houses and thinking how they were all alike, even though they were different colors, and it occurred to me that if somebody's father came home drunk one night he could just as easily go in one house as another and never know the difference. What difference would it make if he went into a pink house or a blue one? The wife who was cooking dinner would be the same, and the kids would be the same, and the dog and the TV. He probably wouldn't even notice.

This thought was so depressing that by the time I reached the old lady's house I was seriously contemplating suicide. There was nobody around, but this glow was coming from the back yard, so I went around to the back. And there was this bonfire of garbage, stinking to high heaven. The old lady, who I had never met before, was throwing cereal boxes into it. She was really weird-looking. Very tiny and frail with bushy white hair and sort of bent over on a cane. But the weird thing was the way she was dressed, because she was wearing a black velvet dress that came down to her ankles. It was pretty ratty-looking and had a couple of holes in it.

"Excuse me," I said. "I've come about the fire."

"Good!" she said. "Splendid blaze, isn't it?"

"What I mean is, my mother sent me about the fire."

"Fine, fine. Is she enjoying it?"

"Well, not exactly ..."

"The Kellogg boxes burn nicely, don't they?"

She was talking as though I were deaf, and on top of everything she had some sort of English accent. Man, did I want to beat a retreat. I could see that I was never going to get through to her.

"Look," I said, "I'm sorry to ruin your fire, but my mother is going to call the police if you don't put it out."

She didn't pay any attention to this, but hobbled up the back steps leaning on her cane. Then she turned and smiled at me. "You're shivering, sir. Come indoors."

I can assure you that the last thing in the universe I wanted to do was to go into this weird old woman's house. The very thought of it depressed me so much that I could have killed myself. However, I am one of those people who never knows how to say no to a thing. So before I knew it, I had gone inside with her.

The inside of her house was fantastic. It was so dilapidated that it looked like it had been designed or something. The ceiling was caving in and the floors were rotted and the fireplace was filled with milk cartons. It was amazing. There was hardly any furniture, and everything was covered with cobwebs and dust. But the really amazing part was that the entire place was stacked with books. On the floor, the tables, everywhere. There must have been a thousand of them.

I was so amazed by all this that I didn't know what to say. I guess it was rude, but I just didn't say anything. What could you say? Lovely place you have here? Meanwhile, she was smiling at me like I had just come off a space ship and needed help. I thought she was going to ask my name and where I lived, and where I went to school and all that. Instead she said,

"Will you join me in a glass of sherry?"

This threw me, because no one had ever asked me such a thing before, and I had never had a drink in my life. I mean, despite my father's drinking, I wasn't particularly interested in alcohol.

"Uh, yes," I said. "Thank you."

"Good! I have an exquisite bottle of Amontillado in the cupboard. Do sit down, sir. The blue chair is the most comfortable."

I sat in the blue armchair and practically went through to the floor because there weren't any springs. Meanwhile, she was limping around in the kitchen and I was getting more suicidal by the moment, wondering what I was doing drinking with someone who was a thousand years old and demented besides.

She brought two glasses and a bottle and sat down in a broken rocker, which was sort of awkward because of her being crippled and everything. It was pretty obvious that she didn't wash much, and her hair was a mess. Yet she was acting like we were in the White House.

"Cheers!" she said, toasting me. So I toasted her back, and then we drank. I really felt miserable.

"What is your opinion of it?" she asked, meaning the sherry.

I thought it tasted like cough syrup. "Well," I said, "I don't know. It's very nice."

She stared at me with these terribly blue eyes. "You are correct. I can see that you are a connoisseur. What would you like to talk about?"

"Well," I said. "I don't know."

"Don't know? How incredible, sir. The universe is filled with wonders, and you don't know what to talk about."

"What would you like to talk about?" I said. Boy, this was really wild. Like something out of *Alice In Wonderland*.

"I will discuss anything that is beautiful," she said.

For a moment I thought she was kidding, but she wasn't. I looked around at all the books. "What about books?"

"Superb! Who is your favorite author?"

"Well, uh, Shakespeare."

"Superb!" she said again. "Which is your favorite play?"

I thought quickly. "*King Lear.*"

"Excellent. Why do you like it?"

She was really putting me on the spot. I gulped some more sherry, and it didn't taste so bad. "Well, I guess I like it because the story is so different. I mean, here's this great king who has everything in the world, yet he has to go crazy just to find out what the score is. The real score, I mean. I mean, he only becomes sane by going crazy first, if you see what I mean."

She nodded. "I certainly do. As a matter of fact, that is the most unusual interpretation of Lear I've ever heard. I shall send it to Sir Laurence Olivier."

"You mean Olivier the actor? The English one and everything?" I had just seen him on television.

"None other. I knew him as a young man at the Old Vic."

I was very surprised. "You mean you were an actress and everything?"

"I do."

"In London and everything?"

She filled my glass up with sherry. "London, Paris, Berlin, Rome. Do stop saying 'and everything', my good man. It doesn't suit you."

"I'm sorry."

"Nothing to be sorry about. But as long as we are speaking English, we may as well speak it beautifully. Don't you agree?"

"Sure," I said. "Why not?"

I was beginning to feel better. "What plays did you act in?"

She sighed and leaned back in her chair. "What plays did I not act in? Shakespeare, Rostand, Chekov, Ibsen, Strindberg, Pinero ..."

"Were you famous?" I asked. I was really getting interested in her.

"Fame is relative," she said. "General de Gaulle is famous. The Beatles are famous. Ivory Liquid Detergent is famous. What does it signify?"

"I don't know."

"'It is a tale told by an idiot, full of sound and fury, signifying nothing.' *Macbeth*. Act Five."

Then she lit a tiny cigar, which surprised me.

I didn't know what to say after that so we just sat there, she smoking this small cigar and me thinking how wild it was, a famous actress living right in the middle of our development. The only person in show business I had ever met was this boy's father who worked in a TV studio. But she wasn't like him at all.

To tell you the truth, I was beginning to feel a bit daring. As though I could say something very wild to her and she would understand. I looked at her, and she seemed different than she had at the beginning. Nicer sort of, and not so insane.

"What is your actual opinion of the soul?" I asked.

She didn't bat an eyelash. "My thoughts about the soul coincide with Bernard Shaw's: '... your soul sticks to you if you stick to it; but the world has a way of slipping through your fingers.' *Heartbreak House*. Act Two."

"Would you mind if I wrote that down?" I said.

"My pleasure," she said. "More sherry?"

I nodded, and she filled my glass again as I wrote the words down in my notebook. I was feeling pretty good. As a matter of fact, the whole decrepit house was looking pretty good. I was really having a very good time.

"Listen," I said suddenly, "this will probably sound insane to you, but I've been feeling like killing myself because my whole life is so lousy. What I mean is, I have a very lousy life and it's nobody's fault but my own."

"Extraordinary," she said. "How do you intend to remedy the problem?"

"I don't know. That's the whole problem. I don't know."

"Why do you think it's your fault?" She really looked interested.

"Well, I don't know. It *seems* to be my fault and everything. I mean, I'm lousy in school and don't fit in anywhere and have all these peculiar tastes that embarrass my mother."

"What do you consider peculiar, sir?"

"You know," I said. "Peculiar."

"No, sir. I do not know."

"Well, like recipes and museums and gardening and the *National Geographic*. You know."

She tapped on the floor with her cane. She looked angry. "All you are saying is that you are different! A quality which puts you in the company of saints and geniuses. Shakespeare was different. Beethoven was different. Plato, St. Francis and Edison were different. Need you complain?"

I had never thought of it that way before. It was fantastic.

"You mean I'm a genius?"

"I have no idea if you are a genius," she said. "However, you do have a certain candor that is refreshing, and your looks are superb."

This really amazed me. "They are?"

"Of course they are! Your features are so sensitive that were I still in the theater I should cast you as Marchbanks. In *Candida*."

I was starting to feel dizzy. I looked at my watch. "Oh man! It's really late. I've got to go. I mean, I don't want to, but I have to."

"Very well," she said. "Come back tomorrow for tea."

"OK. Great. I will."

She reached over and grabbed a table and pulled herself to her feet. Yet all the same it was very graceful.

"My name is Mrs. Orpha Woodfin."

I shook hands with her. "Mine is Albert Scully. How do you do?"

"Do you usually take a large tea?" she asked.

I didn't know what she was talking about, but I said yes.

"Excellent. I shall see you tomorrow at four."

"Excellent," I said. "And listen ..."

She looked up at me with these very blue eyes. "Yes, sir?"

"Burn all the garbage you like. I mean it. Have a ball."

"I shall do that," she said softly, "in the fullness of time. Good night, Mr. Scully."

4 By the time I got home, my mother and father were at the dinner table, which is in the living room. My father was staring at his mashed potatoes and my mother was watching a TV commercial. The Jolly Green Giant was laughing while a lot of elves rushed around with vegetables.

"Where have you been?" my mother asked.

Suddenly I felt very peculiar. As though I were someone in a Cary Grant movie. "To Egypt," I said. "I just came back by camel."

"What?" said my mother.

"There was a sandstorm in the desert, and we were attacked by Arabs. That's why I'm late."

My mother looked at me. "Albert. Come here." I walked over to her and she pulled my head down and sniffed me. "My God. He's been drinking."

"Good," muttered my father.

"Have you been drinking?" she asked. "Have you?" She was pulling on my collar like a madwoman.

"Only a bottle of Amontillado. It was exquisite," I said.

"He's been drinking!" she screamed. "I always knew this would happen. Did that old woman give you liquor? Did she? Say something!"

"The Beatles are famous," I said. "What does it signify?"

"Oh my God," moaned my mother.

"Let him go to bed," said my father. "He'll sleep it off."

My mother grabbed the back of my neck. It really hurt. "Listen to me, Albert. If I ever catch you drinking with that old woman again, I'll lock you up for a year. Do you hear me? Do you?"

"I hear you all too well," I said. "Good night."

"Come back here and have your meat loaf!"

"In the fullness of time," I said. "Good night."

I went into my room and shut the door, and I was sort of laughing to myself because I had never talked back to my mother before and it felt great. In the living room my mother was screaming that now there were *two* alcoholics in the family, but for some reason I didn't care. I just sat down at the typewriter and took out my notebook and typed up Mrs. Woodfin's quotation about the soul. Then I pasted it on the wall over my desk and went to bed with all my clothes on.

Orson settled down on my stomach, tucking his paws under him and purring in this hoarse voice he has. I felt very cheerful, and this feeling was so new that I didn't know what to do with it. I mean, misery is a feeling I have always had room for, but cheerfulness feels crowded if you're not used to it.

Orson was purring like a cement mixer. I rubbed his nose. "Orson," I said, "you have a certain candor that is refreshing, and your looks are superb."

Then I fell asleep.

5 The first thing I did the next morning was to look at myself in the mirror. I looked OK. And the second thing I did was to look at Mrs. Woodfin's quotation about the soul.

... your soul sticks to you if you stick to it; but the world has a way of slipping through your fingers.

Man how true, I thought as I crept into the bathroom. The reason I was creeping was that it was only 5:30 and I wanted to take a long bath before anybody woke up. I realize that baths are supposed to be effeminate and that he-men only take bracing showers, but the truth of the matter is that I like to lie in a hot tub every morning. I take a glass of milk with me and a book, and Orson comes too, and it's a very relaxing way to start the day. If you are a tense person, that is.

So I filled up the tub and eased into it with the *National Geographic*, and Orson lay down on the bathmat. I tried to concentrate on the magazine, but it wasn't long before I was thinking about Mrs. Woodfin. The thought that I was going to see her again was very stimulating. I don't know why. It wasn't just that she was an actress and owned a lot of books. And it wasn't just that she liked Shakespeare. I didn't know what it was.

I ran some more hot water into the tub and Orson got up on his hind legs and peered over the side at me. He always does this when I take a bath, as though he wanted to be sure I weren't drowning. Which only goes to prove that cats are not as indifferent as people think. Cats, as a matter of fact, are terrifically sensitive, only they don't like to show it. Orson put one paw in the water and pulled it out quick. Then he gave me a bored look and lay back down on the bathmat.

There was something about Mrs. Woodfin that was very unusual. Maybe it was her manners. Nobody else had ever called me Mr. Scully before, and I sort of liked it. Then there was the thing she had said about my being "different" and how it put me in the company of saints and geniuses. I had flipped over that because being different was my main problem and she had seen it in about two seconds.

If this isn't too boring, I'll tell you a weird thing that happened to me last fall. I had been thinking about this differentness of mine and what a hangup it was and how I should do something about it. So I decided to go to Greenwich Village. In other words, everyone there is supposed to be really different, and I wanted to make a few friends. So I told my mother that some kids and I were going to the city to see a very educational film and how I would be back on the eleven o'clock bus. If she had known that I was going to Greenwich Village, she would have flipped, but she didn't.

It was Saturday night and the bus to New York was jammed. I was wearing my best suit and tie, and I felt pretty good. I took the West Side subway down to Greenwich Village, and the minute I got out of that subway I could see that the place was swinging. It was fantastic. There were about four million people on the street, and everything was lit up like Palisades Amusement Park. I didn't know my way around very well, so I just started to mingle with the crowd and look at people. And man, were they different. I mean, these were the most different-looking people I had ever seen. The boys had hair down to their shoulders or something, and the girls had on such short skirts that it was almost pornographic. None of this stuff is allowed at my school, so I was very fascinated.

I started to walk east, and the further I walked the more different people became. Some of them were dressed in blankets and bare feet and a lot of them were wearing little bells. And everyone, even the boys, had on beads. There were all these stores along the street, and so I went into one. The merchandise was insane. Incense, light bulbs with flowers in them, pink eyeglasses, Indian toe rings, and a lot of op-art posters that made you dizzy. I couldn't see anything I wanted to buy, but finally I bought a button that said, "Reality Is A Crutch" because it seemed kind of humorous. Then I went into a bookstore that was playing the Beatles so loud you couldn't concentrate on the books, and then I went into an art gallery that didn't have any art in it—just neon lights.

All of a sudden this barefoot girl with long hair and beads came up to me on the street. I thought she was going to say something because she looked so cheerful. But she just gave me a paper flower and walked off laughing to herself. I didn't know what to do with the flower but was afraid to throw it away in case she looked back or something.

To tell you the truth I wasn't having a very good time. Everybody was different and all, but I had no idea how to meet them. Then I saw a coffeehouse that had a sign outside that said "Happening Tonight." I had read about Happenings in *Life* magazine and was sort of curious to see one. So I went inside with my paper flower and sat down at a table. It was so dark that I couldn't see the menu for about five hours, and when I did everything was written in Italian. I didn't know what to order, but finally ordered something called Capuccino which turned out to be coffee and cost a dollar.

Well, the place got very crowded with these hippie people in their blankets, and then all the lights suddenly dimmed—as if they weren't dim enough—and this incredible movie projection flashed on the wall. It was a heart operation, and you could see the heart jumping around with various hands reaching into it. Which was really unpleasant. Then this radio static came on very loud and some insane guy began to run through the audience. Boy, was he a mess. He was half naked and dirty and stank to high heaven. I thought he was going to do something, but all he did was climb up on a ladder and close his eyes. Then a girl with silver hair walked out holding an alarm clock. The clock rang its alarm and she jumped on it until it was broken. Next, a little kid came out and poured a bucket of red-white-and-blue spaghetti on the floor. Meanwhile, this radio static was blaring and the heart operation was still going on. The girl with the silver hair lay down on her back and said the word "usury" five times. Then the little kid covered her with a blanket and the lights came on again and it was over. Boy, was I disappointed. I mean, you could be absolutely certain that something had *happened*, but I didn't know what it was.

I was seriously thinking of leaving when this fantastic guy sat down at my table. Very dirty-looking, with hair to his shoulders and wearing a beat-up army jacket. He had on an earring.

"Hey, man," he said to me.

I wasn't sure what he was getting at, so I just said, "Hey."

"You new around here?"

I decided to play it cool. "Not really."

"Where you from?"

"Oh, here and there," I said. "New Jersey."

He looked surprised. "New *Jersey?*"

"Yeah," I said. "New Jersey."

"How about that?" he said.

He didn't say anything after that, but just put on these pink glasses and stared at me. And the funny thing was, even though I had come to Greenwich Village to meet someone, now that I was meeting them I wasn't too enthusiastic.

"Man?" the guy said.

"Yes?"

"You got any bread on you?"

I thought he was kidding. "How do you mean?"

"You know, man. Bread. B.R.E.A.D."

I was going to make a joke about did he want white or rye, but I didn't.

"I don't get it," I said.

His voice had gone very soft and he was smiling at me. It really made me nervous. "Look man, there are six of us in one pad over on Avenue A and we're very low on grass. So if you have any bread you can smooth us out. Right? Just consider it a little donation to the flower children."

To tell you the truth, I didn't know what he meant. All I knew was that I didn't care how many children he had. I wanted to get out of there.

"Look," I said, getting up from the table, "I'm really very sorry, but I have an appointment with some people in the insurance business."

To make a long story short, I got out of that place and boarded the first subway I saw. I was very depressed on the way home, and finally it occurred to me why. Because these hippie people in Greenwich Village weren't different at all. They looked alike and dressed alike and talked alike. Just like everybody else, but in their own way. What difference did it make whether they had Happenings or stayed home and watched the Ed Sullivan Show? Or whether they had crew cuts or hair to their knees? It didn't make any difference at all. They were just another big organization.

I had been in the bathroom about an hour when I heard people getting up. So I got out of the tub and dressed and went into the kitchen. My mother was pasting Plaid Stamps into a book. She is saving up for an electric can opener.

"How do you feel?" she asked. She looked worried.

"Fine," I said.

And it was true. I didn't even have a hangover.

6 I got to school on time that day and had a pretty good morning. I mean, while it was the same crummy morning I usually have, it didn't seem so bad. All I could think of was that I was going to see Mrs. Woodfin, and for some reason this made me want to fix myself up. So I made several trips to the john to comb my hair. My hair is very soft and uncontrollable and it takes a lot of hairdressing to keep it back. After my third trip, this guy Marvin Williams decided to get cute about it. Which infuriated me because *he* had been in the john all morning, just staring at himself in the mirror.

"Hey, Tarzan," he said. "Still using that greasy kid stuff?"

"Cool it," I said. "Get lost."

"Got a date or something?"

"Yeah," I said. "With Greta Garbo."

Williams was looking at a pimple on his forehead. "What class she in?"

"She's a Sophomore. You know. The redhead with the very good figure. The one who wears a lot of eye makeup."

"Oh yeah," he said. "I've met her a few times."

This shut him up for a while, so when I was sure I looked OK I went to the cafeteria and had lunch. Then came History and Latin and some other stuff I won't bore you with, and by the time it was three o'clock I was very excited. I had told my mother that I had joined the Glee Club and would be home late because of rehearsal. This surprised her so much that she forgot to scold me for being drunk the night before. All of which was very funny, because I couldn't sing a note.

I hung around the baseball field for a while, and went to the library, and combed my hair again, and pretty soon it was time to go. I took the bus to the development and got off at the stop ahead of my house so I wouldn't meet my mother. By the time I reached Mrs. Woodfin's place, it was exactly four o'clock.

I knocked on the door and after a few minutes she opened it. She looked much smaller than I remembered, and a lot messier. She was wearing the same old velvet dress.

"Mr. Scully!" she said. "How good of you to come. I have been anticipating this meeting all day."

"Gee," I said. "So have I."

"Come in, sir. Come in. You must be longing for your tea."

To tell you the truth, I didn't like tea, but the minute I got inside I could see that she had gone to a lot of trouble. There was a whole tea set laid out, and a plate of crackers. A couple of milk cartons were burning in the fireplace.

"Sit down, sir," she said. "Warm yourself by the fire."

I sat down and she lowered herself into the broken rocker and began fussing with the plates and cups. They were pretty filthy, and there was a dead fly in the sugar bowl.

She poured my tea. "Milk or lemon?" she asked.

"Both," I said. It was probably the wrong thing to say, but she didn't let on.

"Splendid. A biscuit?"

I took an old-looking cracker off the plate. "Thank you."

For a few minutes I didn't know what to say. In fact, I wasn't even sure why I had come. I looked at a dilapidated painting over the fireplace. It showed some guy in costume standing by a horse, but his nose was missing. The whole picture was in pretty bad shape.

"Nice picture," I said.

"My grandfather. The Earl Of Arran."

I wasn't sure what an Earl was, so I just sat there wondering why I had come and thinking how different it was to be sober than drunk.

Mrs. Woodfin was staring at me. "Mr. Scully," she said, "I am eighty years old, and when a person reaches that age, formalities are unnecessary. Let us get to the point. Why are you so unhappy?"

This kind of embarrassed me. "How do you mean?"

"You told me yesterday that you were contemplating suicide. This worries and astounds me. I find it unreasonable."

"How do you mean?" I said again.

"You are a highly attractive young man with everything to live for. Suicide is out of the question."

I shrugged. "What would you suggest?"

"Rather than suicide? A great deal. It all depends on your estimation of yourself. Which, I might add, seems rather low."

I picked up a book and pretended to leaf through it, because to tell you the truth I didn't feel like going into this whole thing again. But then there was this long silence, so I said, "Well, you're right. It's low. My estimation, I mean."

"And why is that?"

"I don't know."

"But surely you do, sir."

"Well, I guess it's because I'm a failure or something."

She dropped the cracker she was eating and stared at me like I had just said I was Lee Harvey Oswald. She looked amazed.

"Have I heard you correctly, Mr. Scully?"

"Sure. I guess so"

"I cannot believe my ears! You are literate, sensitive, and intelligent. Yet you tell me that you are a failure."

"Well, it's true," I said. "I am."

"In whose terms?"

"In *everybody's* terms."

"Impossible, sir."

For some reason I was getting a little angry about this. "Look," I said, "here's the picture. I'm a crummy student and a lousy athlete, and I don't have a single friend. I mean, I'm such a mess that I don't even have ambitions. Every other kid in the world has a million ambitions, and I don't. That's the picture."

I thought this would put an end to the subject, but Mrs. Woodfin kept on going.

"Very well. What are their ambitions?"

"They're very good ones!" I said. For some reason my voice had gotten sort of loud. "First off, everybody wants to be popular. That's the first thing. Then they all want to become something important after college. You know. Then I guess they want to be very successful and make a lot of money and get married and live in the suburbs. What's wrong with that?"

She shook her finger at me. "What's wrong with it, Mr. Scully? Everything, simply everything. Those are the deadliest ambitions I ever heard of. Only a coward could admire them."

"Well, I *do* admire them."

"Why?" she asked.

"Why? I don't know why! I just do. And it isn't all so marvelous to be 'different' as you said yesterday. It's lousy."

To be perfectly frank with you, I wasn't behaving very well. Ordinarily I am a very polite person, but Mrs. Woodfin was bugging me so much that I could have walked out on her or something. All of which was crazy, because I hardly knew her.

"Mr. Scully," she said. "Shall I tell you a story?"

"Sure," I said. "Fine." Which wasn't true, because I would have liked to go home.

She looked at me until I looked back, and then she held my eyes with hers.

"When I was your age, Mr. Scully, I had one ambition: to be a great actress. And so I read dozens of plays and recited them before a mirror, turned the attic into a theater, and devised costumes and scenery galore. One day I would be Camille; the next day, Juliet. And all of it seemed very grand, very romantic. Eventually my parents became so weary of this that they sent me to a dramatic academy, where I worked like a fiend. They never suspected I had real talent until my elocution master informed them that I was an exceptional student. I stayed at the academy for two years. And then, sir, on November 1st, 1903, I played Ophelia at the Haymarket Theater—and after the curtain came down the audience unhorsed my carriage and drew it through the streets of London, cheering. From that night on, the horizon of my life was illumined as though by skyrockets. The newspapers called me a young Bernhardt. Managers flocked to my door with contracts. Soon I was acting in every capital of the world and meeting the greatest people of my day: Pavlova, Ibsen, Stanislavsky, Lady Gregory, Yeats, Isadora. It seemed to me that I had achieved everything I had ever longed for. Then, Mr. Scully, the day arrived when I realized that I had achieved everything but happiness—and in one second, the glory turned to dust."

I was kind of bewildered by this. "Well. That's great."

"It was not great at all, sir."

"Look," I said, "you've obviously had a very unusual life, but I'm only a kid. I mean, I live in this crummy development and go to high school, and I have a father who drinks."

She smiled. "Do you know what Rilke said? 'If your daily life seems poor, do not blame it; blame yourself, tell yourself that you are not poet enough to call forth its riches ...' *Letters To a Young Poet.*"

"Would you mind if I wrote that down?" I asked.

"My pleasure," said Mrs. Woodfin.

I don't know how long we talked after that. It must have been hours. I calmed down and told her my whole life, and she listened like she was really interested. Then she told me some more about her life, and I had to admit that it had been unusual.

She had grown up in a place called Bloomsbury in London, and her father had been a famous explorer. She had become an actress when she was only sixteen, and had acted everywhere in the world. She had traveled around in a special railroad car and had been admired by everybody. Kings, queens, everybody. Famous writers had written plays for her. Big-time painters had painted her picture. But for some reason she had given up acting in her twenties and moved to America, where she had lost a lot of money in the stock market crash. New Jersey was like the country then, with no developments, and so she had bought this house in order to live simply and enjoy Nature and everything. It was fantastic. Here was a famous person who had had everything in the world and given it up because it didn't make for "happiness." I couldn't understand it.

Well, by the time I left her house I felt drunk again. Only this time it was a kind of mental drunkenness. Something had really shook me up, and though I wasn't positive what it was, I had this strange feeling that I was going to find out.

7 The next day was Saturday, which is a pretty dull day at our place. My mother fixes herself up to play bridge and my father fixes the house. Personally, I have always felt that he would rather sleep on Saturday, but my mother nags him to do things that she reads about in *House Beautiful.*

This Saturday wasn't any different. My father was out in the back yard trying to build a barbecue pit, and my mother was sitting under her portable hair drier painting her nails with a color called Peach Tease. The TV was going, and the kitchen radio, and the blender and the washing machine. All in all, it was pretty noisy.

I didn't feel like going to the library, so I just hung around the house thinking about Mrs. Woodfin, and for some reason I was depressed. I tidied my room and put my laundry in the hamper, and then I went into the bathroom to run a tub. I figured that I would lie there for a while and read *Othello.* I realize that it is peculiar of me to like Shakespeare, but the reason I like him is that once you get past the old-fashioned language, his plots are very human.

My mother had gotten out from under the hair drier and was heading for the kitchen. Suddenly she screamed.

"What is it?" I called.

"No!" she screamed. "Oh, no!"

I thought she had hurt herself or something, so I dashed out of the bathroom and ran into the kitchen. My mother was sitting at the kitchen table with her head in her hands, and there was about a gallon of vegetable juice running down the wall.

"What happened?" I said.

"The top came off the blender."

It was true. The plastic top had broken, and this health-drink she had been making had gone into orbit. It was a mess. Celery juice, tomato juice, and carrot juice all over the place. The kitchen looked like a modern painting.

"My whole life has been like this," said my mother. "My whole rotten life. Get your father."

I could see that an argument was coming, but I didn't want to interfere so I went out to the yard. My father was on his knees by the barbecue pit and he was mumbling to himself. I stood and watched him for a minute. All the bricks he had laid were crooked and he was up to his elbows in cement.

"Dad?" I said.

"Go away," he said.

"Mom wants you."

He didn't seem to hear me. Then I noticed that he had a glass of Coke with him. Whenever he carries a glass of Coke around it means it has liquor in it. I went back to the kitchen. "He's coming," I said. Then I went into my room and looked at the new quotation over my desk.

If your daily life seems poor, do not blame it; blame yourself, tell yourself that you are not poet enough to call forth its riches ...

I lay down on the bed and wondered who this guy Rilke was, and how he ever could have had a thought like that. My daily life had been awful from the day I was born, and becoming a poet wasn't going to help. On top of which, I just couldn't dig what

Mrs. Woodfin had said about my admiring deadly ambitions. Just because I was a total failure didn't mean that everyone else's ambitions were wrong. And while I wasn't a very joyful person, I had been sort of used to being a failure. Now everything had changed, and I didn't know what to do about it. I mean, what was I supposed to do? Become a hippie or something?

But when I told Mrs. Woodfin that I didn't have any ambitions, it wasn't exactly true. I did have one. Only it was such a peculiar one that I didn't have the guts to tell anybody. You see, my uncle lived for a while in this modern apartment house near the George Washington bridge, and every time I would go there I would look out of his picture window and watch the tugboats on the Hudson River. And it was really beautiful. Especially at night. These little old tugboats would glide by all lit up with lights, and they would seem so peaceful that I would imagine I was a sailor on one of them. Not the captain or anything. Just a sailor. And I would think what a great life it would be just to ride up and down the Hudson River on one of those tugboats and stand on the deck at night and watch the skyline of New York. It wouldn't even matter if the tugboat was pushing a garbage scow. The great thing would be to be there, just a sailor, but a peaceful sailor who knew that nobody was going to bug him to do anything more important. This writer I liked called Thoreau would have understood, because *he* never got anywhere in life. But then I would think of how my mother would feel, especially with her friends. "What is Albert doing these days? Going to Princeton?" they would ask. "No, he's pushing garbage up and down the Hudson," she would say. And she would be boiling inside, because she has always wanted me to be educated and make money. Which is why she is so hot on college and so down on the insurance business.

I don't think I've mentioned this before, but I had a kind of nervous breakdown when I was eight years old. My grandfather had died and left some money, so my mother decided to spend it on me. If she had spent it in the sense of buying me a bike or a telescope, it might have been OK. But she didn't. Instead, she said that she was now ready to give me certain "advantages" I hadn't had before. These were the advantages: piano lessons, dancing lessons, swimming lessons, and horseback riding lessons. In addition to which she enrolled me in the Cub Scouts. Well, that was a pretty wild year. Here I was trying to attend grammar school and at the same time carrying a schedule that would have worried LBJ. All I did was hurry from lesson to lesson, and the more I did this the more upset I became. I mean, I was so tired that I began to cry all the time and have insomnia. Because in addition to failing grammar school, I was now failing all these lessons. Either I would be falling off a horse at the Wildwood Stables or drowning in the pool at the YMCA, or stepping all over some girl's feet at the dancing school. The piano teacher lived forty-five minutes away from our house, and no sooner would I get home from that lesson than it would be time for the Cub Scouts. I was really upset, and eventually my mother had to take me to the doctor because I was getting this ringing in my ears. The doctor examined me and told my mother that I was the first eight-year-old he had ever seen who was having a nervous breakdown, and that she had better stop all these lessons. So she stopped them, except for the piano lessons. But I don't think she ever got over the disappointment.

I lay there thinking these things until I noticed that Orson was sitting in the closet again. In the dark. About two years ago he caught a mouse in there and never recovered from it. So now he spends a part of each day just sitting there as though the same old mouse were going to come back. Orson is one of the few people in the world that I like, but this habit of his irritates me.

"Orson," I said. "Get out of there." He didn't move.

I got up and took him out of the closet, and then I read the quotation from Rilke again. Suddenly I had this idea. So I sat down at my desk and wrote Mrs. Woodfin a letter.

> *Dear Mrs. Woodfin,* (it said)
> *I have been trying to call forth the riches of my daily life, but I guess I'm not a poet because it hasn't worked so well, and as you said I've been admiring deadly ambitions. Anyway, thank you for the tea. It was very nice.*
> *Sincerely,*
> *Albert Scully*

I took the letter and went out to the back yard. My father wasn't there and my mother didn't seem to be around, so I picked some daffodils. It was April, and these flowers I had planted were starting to come up. Then I walked over to Mrs. Woodfin's house and left the flowers and the letter by her door. I guess it was a way of saying good-bye, because something in me never wanted to see her again, or talk about ambition, or find out anything I didn't already know.

But it was funny, because on the way home I felt more depressed than ever.

8 I spent the next few days trying not to think about Mrs. Woodfin, but it didn't work very well. No sooner would I put her out of my mind than she would jump in again. I kept seeing her in this shabby old dress, living in this decrepit house, and still being cheerful about it and having good manners and everything. And I kept thinking how hard it must be to be poor when you had once been rich and famous. But to tell you the truth, the thing she had said about my being a coward had hurt my feelings. I had spent my whole life trying to live up to what people expected of me, and if that made me a coward then I was a coward.

On the other hand, I was sort of a coward in certain areas. And if you came right down to it I didn't even have a good character. I had known this for a long time because my mother was always telling me so. She had a real obsession about character and was always saying that the best example of no character was my father. Which I didn't agree with, because I thought my father was making the best of a pretty hard situation.

The reason I was thinking about character was that I had just done something I hadn't done for years. Which was to steal from the Western Auto Store. I hadn't stolen anything since I was twelve, but two days after I left the note at Mrs. Woodfin's I walked right into Western Auto and stole a box of carpet tacks. I hadn't known that I was going to steal it, and I didn't want it in the first place, but when I saw it on the shelf this uncontrollable impulse had come over me and I had slipped it in my pocket.

There were some other things that were wrong with my character too. I had some very immoral daydreams connected with sex, which I won't go into here, and I was a terrible liar. If anyone at school even asked me how I was, I would go into a long song and dance about how I had just had pneumonia and was making a slow recovery. I even used to pull this stuff in the first grade, when I would put a bandage on my leg and limp around at recess. Not so long ago the postman asked me where my mother was because he had a package for her. "She's flown to Washington," I said. "A government job." The postman was very impressed. "Terrific," he said. "Terrific." The trouble was, I could pull all these things and people were so gullible that they believed them.

I tried to think of what else was wrong with my character, but outside of stealing and lying and sex, I couldn't think of anything. But it didn't matter, because these things were enough to ruin me for the rest of my life, and I knew it. Maybe my character was the thing that had made me such a failure. I just didn't know.

Anyway, it was spring and the Dairy Queen had opened again, so I decided to drown my sorrows in food. It was Tuesday, and as soon as school was over, I took the bus to the development and walked over to the Dairy Queen and ordered a hot fudge and marshmallow sundae. I was just about to dig into it when this old Chevy drove up and Herbie Steiner got out of it with four other guys. And in one second, that sundae lost its appeal. It's like this. Of all the kids in my school, bar none, Herbie Steiner is the most popular. He is so popular that you could imagine him being President one day—and he is only a

Junior. He is a good student and *also* a good athlete. He doesn't break rules, but gives the impression that he is always about to. He is terribly polite to girls but very raucous with boys. What I am trying to say is, Herbie Steiner fits in everywhere.

You see, no matter who you are in my school, you at least belong to one group. Either you belong to the hoods who are the leather-jacket types who get into trouble, or you belong to the athletes who wear white socks everywhere. Or you belong to the squares who do nothing but study and get good grades. Or finally, you belong to the kids who pretend to be hippies. You know. The kind who wear old clothes and discuss LSD like they took it every minute. But the point is, Herbie Steiner fits in with all these groups. On top of which, he has about four thousand extracurricular activities. He belongs to the Dramatics Club and the Glee Club and the French Club and the Chess Club. Any other kid would have a nervous collapse doing all these things, but not Herbie Steiner. As a matter of fact, all you have to do is look at him and you know immediately that he is going to be a fabulous success in life.

To tell you the truth, I have always admired Herbie Steiner. So when he got out of that car, my own situation with Mrs. Woodfin came crashing down on my head like a brick. I just couldn't believe that she was right about failure and success, because the biggest success I knew was standing right there before my eyes, and he looked terrific. He was wearing faded levis and boots and a jacket with the name of our school on it, and his hair was sort of tousled. Herbie looks a little like Rock Hudson and has a very good build. But even though he was wearing these clothes, you could be sure that in another situation he would be wearing a completely different set of clothes. I mean, if he was going to a party at a girl's house, he would be wearing a very conservative suit, and if he was going swimming with the guys he would be wearing some very loud trunks and a battered old hat.

Herbie and his friends ordered their ice cream and started horsing around, and you could tell what a good time they were having. They didn't notice me, so I just stood and watched them and after a while they sat down on a bench and ate their ice cream and started to discuss college. The other four guys wanted to go to places like N.Y.U. and Fordham, but Herbie was set on Yale. And you knew right away that not only would he get into Yale but be the most popular student Yale ever had.

After a few minutes they noticed me. "Hey," said one of the guys. "There's Scully."

"Scully who?" said another guy.

"You know," said the first guy. "Scully. Hey Scully, how's the gardening?"

Well, I just stood there paralyzed, because this first guy, whose name was Larry Weld, lived on my block and had seen me gardening once in the back yard.

"How's the gardening, Scully?" he asked. "I mean, how are your petunias, man?"

Normally I could have said something to shut him up, but the fact that Herbie Steiner was listening paralyzed me. Not that I could ever have been a friend of Herbie Steiner, but I didn't want him to think of me as a gardener.

Larry Weld was really enjoying himself. "What's the matter, man? You gone deaf or something? I want to know about your petunias. And I especially want to know about your pansies."

They all started to laugh at this, so I did the only thing I could. Which was to walk away. But all the way down that block I could hear them laughing, and the most terrible part of it was that Herbie Steiner was laughing, too.

Orson was sitting on the front steps when I got home. He

pretended not to notice me, but I knew that he had. I picked him up and slung him over my shoulder and just held him.

"Orson," I said. "I need help."

And the minute I said that, I knew what to do.

9 "It was 1906," Mrs. Woodfin was saying, "and I had been invited to play Juliet in Paris. At the Ode on Theater. It was a thrilling invitation because Madame Sarah Bernhardt—the most famous actress in the world—had just played the role at the same theater. The tension was extreme. Here was I, a novice from another country, about to invade the artistic territory of the 'Divine Sarah' as Oscar Wilde called her."

"Were you scared?" I asked.

We were out in Mrs. Woodfin's yard, and it was Wednesday afternoon. I had cut school. Not just a few classes, but the whole day. Mrs. Woodfin was sitting on a barrel, and I was sitting on the grass.

"Scared, Mr. Scully? I was elated. Madame Sarah was sixty-two years old. I was nineteen. I had everything in my favor: youth, beauty, naiveté, talent. In addition to which, I had decided to play the role in French."

"Man!" I said. "What happened?"

"It was a gorgeous spring evening, the kind you only have in Paris, and the theater was crowded. A special box had been reserved for Bernhardt, but she did not enter it until the curtain was up and the play began. This gesture was typical of her temperament, her vanity. Romeo was speaking, and the poor man's lines were almost obliterated by the spectacle of Madame

Sarah's entrance. She swept into her box like a queen. She nodded to the audience, she smiled, she fluttered her fan. And everyone's eyes were upon her. It was obvious that those of us on the stage were in for a contest."

"Man," I said. "Who won?"

"Wait and I shall tell you. I had begun the play badly, because of nervousness. My voice was unsteady and my hands were trembling. But by the time the third act arrived, I was in glorious command."

Mrs. Woodfin grabbed the sides of the barrel and pushed herself to her feet. Then she leaned on her cane and gazed into the distance with these very blue eyes she has. And it gave me chills, because suddenly she looked young.

"'Come gentle night …'" she said. "'Give me my Romeo; and, when he shall die, take him and cut him out in little stars, and he will make the face of heaven so fine that all the world will be in love with night and pay no worship to the garish sun …' From that moment on, Mr. Scully, the evening was mine. Not a sound could be heard in that theater, and when the final curtain came down there was no applause. People were too stunned to applaud. And then Madame Sarah Bernhardt, the Divine Sarah, the greatest actress in the world, rose to her feet and shouted, 'Bravo!' Her clarion voice rang through the theater and was followed by a thousand voices shouting 'Bravo, Bravo, Bravo.'"

Mrs. Woodfin stopped and stared at me. "Mr. Scully, why aren't you in school?"

I had been so interested in her story that I had to shake myself awake. "What?"

"You are not in school today, sir. Is it possible that you are playing truant?"

"Well, yes," I said. "It's possible."

"In that event, you are defying the law."

I pulled a dandelion and started to pick it apart. "Yes, I guess I am."

Mrs. Woodfin eased herself down on the barrel. "You must have a good reason to do such a thing. Would you like to discuss it?"

I glanced at her to see if she was kidding, but her face was serious. She was wearing the same old dress with the holes in it but she looked nice all the same. Pretty, sort of.

"It's very simple," I said. "I just haven't been able to concentrate very much since we had tea and everything. I mean, what you said about my being a coward sort of bothered me. That's all."

"In other words, I hurt your feelings."

"Well, yes. Sure."

She leaned down and took my hand, which surprised me. Her hand was very cool. "I am sorry for that, Mr. Scully. You must forgive me."

"I do. Honest," I said.

She was still holding my hand, and it sort of embarrassed me. So I changed the subject.

"What happened after everyone yelled bravo?" I asked. "Weren't you thrilled?"

"Thrilled, sir? I was ecstatic. I took my curtain calls and ran back to my dressing room and danced for joy. Boxes of flowers were arriving, champagne was flowing, people were swarming round my door. Then a hush fell over the crowd as Bernhardt herself walked into the room. Her eyes were moist, and as she embraced me she murmured, 'Mon ange, mon ange.' We both wept then. She, because my Juliet had moved her. I, because I had just seen true generosity for the first time in my life. Little did I know, however, what a really valiant woman she was.

54

Within a few years her leg would be amputated and she would still carry on—entertaining the troops on the battlefields of World War I. Yes, Mr. Scully, that night in Paris was my greatest triumph. And yet, four years later I left the theater and never acted again."

I gripped her hand, because all of a sudden I wanted to get through to her. To explain. I had never wanted anything so much in my life.

"But don't you see?" I said. "It was easy for you to leave the theater because you'd been there. Don't you see? You'd made it. But I've never made anything. Nobody admires me or even likes me. That's the worst part. If somebody just liked me, I'd feel better. But all I do is walk around like Frankenstein's monster. And everyone is after me to get with it. And the more they tell me to get with it, the more paralyzed I become. It's awful."

"What do they want you to get with?" Mrs. Woodfin asked. Her voice was very calm.

"I don't know! That's the worst part. I don't know. I mean, I do know in a way. What they're talking about is the world. Going to college and being a success and making money. Joining things. Everywhere you turn people are telling you to join things. Haven't you ever listened to them? Join the Pepsi Generation! Go where the action is! Be a swinger! Make the scene! That's what they want you to do. All of them."

"And what do *you* want to do, Mr. Scully?"

I didn't know what to say. Because outside of being a sailor on a tugboat or moving to New Zealand, I didn't know. I looked at Mrs. Woodfin, and she seemed really interested. It wasn't like she was talking to a kid or anything. She really wanted to find out. And the fact that she was so interested brought these lousy tears to my eyes.

"Look," I said, "I'm the only person in America who doesn't

belong to a group. I'm not square and I'm not hip. I'm not a hood. I'm not an intellectual. I'm not an athlete. And what else is there?"

"What else, sir? Why, yourself. Have you ever thought of just being yourself?"

Well, this one stopped me cold. Dead cold. Because I never had thought of it.

"No," I said.

Mrs. Woodfin turned my hand over in hers. We had been holding hands for a long time now, and my hand was sweating.

"There is a beautiful Jewish proverb," she said. "'If I am not for myself, who will be for me? And if I am only for myself, what am I?' It was written by a person named Hillel."

I didn't know who Hillel was, and to tell you the truth I didn't care.

"Well, I guess he didn't know anything about the Pepsi Generation," I said.

"He knew a great deal about it! My dear young man, can't you see that every era has had its Pepsi Generations? The Greeks had them, and the Egyptians had them, and the Elizabethans had them. There will always be a Pepsi Generation for those who want to join it. But you, quite obviously, don't want to join anything. Correct?"

I sighed. "Correct. One hundred per cent correct. That's why I'm such a mess."

I was starting to feel tired. Because I wasn't digging her, and the whole thing seemed so hopeless that I just felt like going off and committing suicide. Here was Mrs. Woodfin telling me to be myself, when myself was the thing that was wrong with me. As a matter of fact, I hadn't even been wanted in the first place. Which was why the whole mess started. My mother hadn't wanted any children, and the only reason I got into the world was through bad planning. I had overheard her discussing this once with my father, and I had never forgotten it.

Suddenly Mrs. Woodfin stared over the back fence. I looked where she was looking, but all I could see was a United Parcel truck delivering a package to someone's house. For a moment I thought she was going to recite another Jewish proverb. But what she said was this:

If a man does not keep pace with his companions, perhaps it is because he hears a different drummer. Let him step to the music which he hears, however measured or far away.

And that was the very moment when I dug her.

"*Walden!*" I said. "By Thoreau. *Henry David Thoreau!*"

10 I slipped in the back door around five o'clock and went straight to my room so I could think about Thoreau. It was amazing. I had read Walden about a million times, yet I had never noticed that quotation about the drummer. It was the best quotation I had ever heard, and I had never noticed it. Which made me wonder what else I hadn't been noticing. Thoreau himself, maybe. I mean, when you read a lot of books you don't necessarily feel that you know the authors. They just seem like distant relations. But there was Thoreau living in the woods because he heard a different drummer, and here was Mrs. Woodfin living in New Jersey for the same reason. In other words, here were two very happy dropouts that I knew personally.

It's odd, but I had always thought of Thoreau as a failure. Which is why I had read his book so many times. He had once been a pencil-maker and had made the best pencil the world had ever known, and then given the whole thing up. Anyone else would have gone on to make a killing in pencils, but old Thoreau just stopped making them and went off to live at Walden Pond in Massachusetts. Which had seemed incredible to me. But now I saw why. It was because of that drummer.

Suddenly it occurred to me that I had cut school that day. So I slipped into the hall to see what my mother was doing. It didn't seem that anyone from school had phoned because she was just lying on the living room couch reading *Valley Of The Dolls*. I tried to read *Valley Of The Dolls* once too, but couldn't because it is so badly written. My mother had her hair in rollers, and she looked very absorbed.

I went back to my room and typed up Thoreau's quotation and pasted it on the wall. Then I sat at my desk for a while. I didn't feel depressed and I didn't feel happy. I just felt expectant—like I used to feel on Christmas when I was little. We had had some pretty good Christmases in those days because my mother hadn't been so irritable. Once she had even gotten my uncle to dress up as Santa Claus for me, and I had really enjoyed it. It was corny and everything, but when you're little, corny things are nice.

We had dinner at seven-thirty, and my mother was in a very chatty mood because she and my father were going to the movies. Something with Elizabeth Taylor in it. My mother always ignored Elizabeth Taylor until she married Richard Burton, but now she is very concerned with their marriage and talks about them like they were relatives. She talks about a lot of people that way, which always strikes me as funny because she is so concerned with all these people she doesn't know. Take Lady Bird Johnson. You would think that she and my mother were sisters because she is constantly criticizing her clothes and her manners and her accent and everything. What I mean is, my mother is more concerned with Lady Bird Johnson than with my father. My father could wear a red-white-and-blue striped suit, and she wouldn't notice. But just let Lady Bird Johnson wear a funny-looking dress and my mother goes insane.

Anyway, the dinner hour wasn't bad and my parents got out of the house by eight forty-five. Which meant that I could be alone and think. So I went out and sat on the back steps, and Orson came with me. There was a full moon in the sky, and the night was very cool with a smell of flowers in it. All the houses in the development were lit up and they looked sort of pretty and unreal. It's strange how pretty the development can look at times. See it in the daytime and it's boring. But watch it on a clear spring night and you could almost imagine you were in another country. I often sit on the back steps at night and pretend that I'm in Wellington, New Zealand. If I squint I can almost see an imaginary harbor all circled with lights. It's funny how much I love New Zealand. I've been dreaming about it for years.

Mrs. Woodfin had said that I should just be myself and forget about joining things. Which was a wild idea, because if I did that my whole life would probably collapse. On the other hand, it was rather collapsed already. It was a strange situation: me, Thoreau and his pencils, and Mrs. Woodfin in her decrepit house. But even though Mrs. Woodfin's ideas were far-out, at least she listened to your ideas, which is something older people rarely do. My mother, for example, is always telling me to express myself, but the minute I try to express myself she jumps in with her own opinions and I know right away that she hasn't heard anything I've expressed. Whereas Mrs. Woodfin treated you like an equal, even though she was from England and had a better vocabulary than yours.

But that part about the drummer was really beautiful. I thought about it until I went to bed.

11 It was nine o'clock the next morning and I was sitting in English class. In other words, my body was sitting there but my mind was far away. Mr. Finley, the teacher, was discussing *To Kill A Mockingbird* and the whole thing was so boring that I had stopped listening. No matter what book we read in English, it is always a story about youth going through experience and improving itself. Southern youth. Northern youth. European youth. To judge from these books you would think that youth did nothing but go through experience and come out great at the end. If Mr. Finley ever gave us a book in which youth went to pieces at the end, I would be more interested.

I stared at Mr. Finley to make him think I was listening, and then I let my mind drift over to Mrs. Woodfin. It was strange that we had got onto the subject of joining things yesterday, because a month before I met her I had tried to join something very hard. And failed, of course. But the point is I had tried, and her words had brought the whole experience back to me. You see, any kid in our school who gets into trouble is sent to the Psychologist, and one Monday morning my homeroom teacher said that this Psychologist wanted to see me. So I went to his office, which is near the gym, and I was sort of nervous because I couldn't imagine what I had done. I had never met a Psychologist before, so I was surprised to find this one very youthful-looking with blond hair. He was wearing slacks and a sweater and horn-rimmed glasses.

"Hi there, Scully," he said. "Have a seat, man."

Well, the minute he said "man" I knew something was up, because none of the other teachers use that expression.

"My name is Chuck Forbes. Helluva nice day, isn't it?"

I shook hands with him. "Yes, sir. It is."

We both sat down and the whole thing was very peculiar, because it was like we were at a party or something.

"Cool jacket you're wearing," he said.

"Thank you," I said. And then there was this long pause.

"Scully," he said, "I sent for you because we've got a hang-up here."

"Oh? What's that, sir?"

He took off his glasses and grinned at me. "Come on, now. Don't give me that 'sir' stuff. You know what the hang-up is."

"My grades?" I asked.

"Well sure, man. Your grades are part of it. But I've been studying your Personality Evaluation Card, and I don't think grades are the whole problem."

By now I was feeling pretty nervous. "What is it then? Have I done something?"

He crinkled his eyes, which made him look like Van Johnson in one of those old movies on the Late Show. "Let's say it's what you haven't done. All the comments on this Evaluation Card add up to one thing: you're a loner."

"Oh," I said. "Well, yes. I guess that's true."

"Do you like being a loner, Scully?"

"It's OK. It's not so bad, really."

"I don't agree with you, man. No kid likes to be a loner. That's what's got your teachers all hung up. Actually, they're very worried about you."

"Well, that's very nice of them," I said.

"I don't think you're digging me, Scully. What your teachers want you to do is get with the action a little more. Swing with the other kids. They think that if you participate in school life a little more, your grades will improve. Dig?"

"Sure," I said. "Of course." But the truth of the matter is that I wasn't fooled by him at all because he was about the biggest phony I had ever met. There he sat looking like Van Johnson and using all these slang words when he was probably a Ph.D. from Harvard. I could just see him sneaking into school every morning in a business suit and changing into those old slacks in the john.

"What would you like me to do?" I asked.

He was still grinning at me. "That, man, is entirely up to you. But if I were in your place, I would try to make the scene and do something groovy. You know. Go to a few dances, join a few clubs. Being cool is one thing, but a guy can be *too* cool. Dig?"

To make a long story short, I told him that I dug him and that I would participate a little more, and then I got out of there. And all the way back to class I kept thinking how much I hated older people who tried to pretend that they were on your side, when all they were doing was giving you the axe.

On the other hand, what he had said about my being a loner was true. I didn't like it. So I decided to try and participate for a change. There was going to be a dance at school called "The Tramp's Ball" which everyone was looking forward to because it meant you could wear old clothes. This very well-known rock 'n' roll group called The Trash Cans was going to play, too. So I decided to go.

My mother was pleased when I told her, because I had always refused to go to dances in the past. I was sort of worried about my costume, but she was very nice about it and helped me put one together. First we got an old pair of my father's pants that had some patches in them, and then we found a torn red-and-green checked shirt in the basement. Next we put some red suspenders on the pants, and then my mother loaned me her straw gardening hat. I tried on all this stuff in front of the mirror and it looked pretty good.

The dance was on a Friday night, and my father had to drive me there because I felt self-conscious about going on the bus. But he let me off a block from the school, so no one would see that he had driven me. The dance was being held in the cafeteria, and as I walked down the hall I could hear that it had already started. I was feeling pretty excited because of my costume and everything, but the minute I got to the cafeteria I could see that I had made a terrible mistake. A really terrible mistake. No one was dressed as a tramp. I mean, not a single person. The boys were just wearing old levis and shirts, and the girls were wearing these very dressy pantsuits. I must have looked like something out of Halloween, because around a hundred people turned and stared at me.

I couldn't imagine how I had made such a mistake, so I just stood there feeling paralyzed. The Trash Cans were playing up on a platform and everyone was dancing. There were tables against the walls with candles on them, and a refreshment stand had been set up near the door.

My first impulse was to go home. But then I thought of how disappointed my mother would be, so I sat down at an empty table. I was really feeling awful, because outside of the fact that I wasn't a very good dancer, I saw that I was the only person in the school who had taken the theme of the dance literally. Which is just like me. However, the table I was sitting at was rather dark, so I decided to just stay there and be inconspicuous.

By now you may have guessed that I am not the kind of person who likes rock 'n' roll, and these people called The Trash Cans were not about to change my opinion. They were really unattractive: six guys with hair to their shoulders and dressed in tight velvet pants and lace shirts. They looked around sixteen years old and were so girlish that I was almost embarrassed. Their music was the worst stuff I had ever heard. Very un-lyrical and so loud that you couldn't understand the words. Every so often you could make out that they were saying "yeah, yeah" or "man, man" but that was all. I guess I am the only kid in America who doesn't like this kind of music, but the reason I don't like it is because it is fickle. No sooner do you get to understand rock 'n' roll than it turns into folk-rock. And no sooner do you try to dig that than it becomes soul-music. In fifty years no one will remember it at all, which is something you could never say for Brahms.

I sat there listening to this terrible music and watching everyone on the dance floor making fools of themselves when Miss Ashburn sat down at my table. Miss Ashburn is my Latin teacher, and for some reason she has this big thing about me—which is very peculiar considering how lousy I am in Latin. But for six months her whole mission in life has been to make friends with me, and it's really embarrassing because she comes on so strong.

"Albert!" she said. "How good to see you, dear. Are you having a good time? Can I get you anything?"

"No," I said. "Thank you. I'm fine."

"Isn't it a lovely dance? And I think your costume is just marvelous. So realistic. Are you supposed to be dressed as Charlie Chaplin?"

"No," I said.

Fortunately this conversation didn't go any farther because

my Algebra teacher came up and asked her to dance. So I was left alone again, and by now I was really feeling miserable. Not that people were still staring at me. But I felt like they were, which is just as bad. I couldn't have asked anyone to dance if they had offered me a million bucks.

I looked across the room and saw Herbie Steiner doing a dance called the shingaling with Alice Ridgely. Alice is a cheerleader and the most beautiful girl in the school so of course she and Herbie go steady. They are very serious about each other and kiss in public, and many people say that they are making out. Which in this instance I believe, because Herbie is a very persuasive guy.

Well, after a half hour I discovered that I just couldn't go on sitting there, so I took off my straw hat and edged over to the refreshment stand to get a Coke. And then I saw Clarence Trautmann, who is a Sophomore and is called The Trout by everybody because he is such a clod. He is almost more of a clod than I am, so I decided to talk to him. I mean, here I was at a dance and everything, and I had no one to talk with. So I figured that it would at least be safe to talk to Trautmann. He was standing against the wall munching a bag of potato chips, and his pimples looked worse than ever.

"Hi," I said.

He looked at my costume in a funny way but didn't say anything about it. "Hi."

"What do you think of the dance?" I was pretty sure he didn't like it, so I felt safe in asking. But he surprised me.

"Cool," he said. "The Cans are in great form tonight."

"Oh," I said. "You mean you like them and everything?"

"I think they're fabulous."

His mouth was so full of potato chips that he could hardly talk, and for some reason this irritated me.

66

"You must be off your rocker," I said. "I think they're terrible."

"Why?" asked Trautmann.

"Why? Because they stink, that's why."

"They don't stink at all."

"They *do* stink. They look like girls, and they're noisy, and you can't understand a word they say. I mean, if somebody would just play a little Brahms once in a while, the culture of this country might improve."

Trautmann turned and looked at me with the strangest look I had ever seen. It really made me go cold, because it was a very pitying look that was mixed with happiness. As if he had finally discovered somebody in the whole universe who was stupider than he was.

"Scully," he said to me, "has it ever occurred to you that you can't dance to Brahms?"

12

"And so he turned and gave me this pitying look and said that you can't dance to Brahms."

"What did you say?" asked Mrs. Woodfin.

"That's the trouble. I couldn't say anything. Because he had a point. You can't dance to Brahms."

"Why should one have to?" she asked.

Well, of course she was right. Brahms had never wanted to compose dance music in the first place, and the minute she said that I saw how stupid Trautmann's comment had been. That was the thing about Mrs. Woodfin. She got to the heart of the matter right away.

It was Friday afternoon, and I was back at Mrs. Woodfin's house. This time I had told my mother that I would be late from school because of joining the Dramatics Club, and she had really been pleased. But it was funny, because even though my last meeting with Mrs. Woodfin had been sort of emotional, I hadn't been embarrassed to come back. And now we were getting along like nothing had happened—she drinking sherry at the kitchen table, and me sitting on a wooden stool drinking tea. Mrs. Woodfin's kitchen would be a shock to some people, but it wasn't to me. I mean, while the sink was dirty, and the linoleum rotted away, and the ceiling coming down, it was still cheerful. There were tulips in a tomato juice jar and a whole set of Dickens on top of the refrigerator.

I had come to the door that afternoon without any warning, but she hadn't been surprised. She had just invited me into the kitchen and given me a cup of tea, and it wasn't long before we were talking about Thoreau. I told her how I had dug that quotation about the drummer, and then she told me some more about Thoreau's life. It was amazing how much Mrs. Woodfin knew about him even though she was a foreigner. I had never realized, for example, why Thoreau hated possessions, but Mrs. Woodfin said it was because he considered them hindrances to the development of the human spirit. Looking around the kitchen you could see that she agreed with him, because she didn't even own a toaster.

We talked for about an hour, and I told her all about "The Tramp's Ball," and then she asked if I would like to take a tour of the house and grounds. At first I thought she was putting me on, but when I saw that she wasn't, I followed her out to the yard. It was surprising how well she got around in spite of being crippled. She would just lean on her cane with one hand and grab onto pieces of furniture with the other, and propel herself that way.

I had seen the yard at least three times, but I pretended like I hadn't because she seemed to enjoy showing it to me so much. "The northeast corner is the most interesting," she said. So we walked over to the northeast corner, which had a pile of trash in it, and looked out over the development. "Nice view," I said, half kidding. But she took me seriously. "You are correct, Mr. Scully. This is the best view from the property. The sunsets are superb."

We stomped around the yard for a while, looking at all the different corners and views, and then she showed me her "garden." It was a pretty pathetic sight because it was filled with weeds and only had four or five flowers in it. But she didn't seem to see how pathetic it was because she said how magnificently the tulips were doing this year.

By the time we got back to the house, I was feeling sort of baffled. Because she wasn't kidding. She really *did* think her place was attractive. And the more she showed me around the more baffled I became. First there was the kitchen, which I have already described, and then there was the living room, which had nothing in it but stacks of books and a few pieces of broken furniture. Then there was a very drab-looking bathroom with no tub, and last of all a tiny little bedroom with only a bed and a bureau and some old photos on the wall. They were all of people I had never heard of—like Henry Irving and Ellen Terry and Mrs. Patrick Campbell. I guess what I was looking for were things like TV sets and phonographs, but as far as I could see, Mrs. Woodfin didn't even own a radio. She certainly owned the *New York Times*, though. There were about a thousand copies of it in the hall.

After the tour we sat down by the fireplace, which as usual was filled with milk cartons, and she asked me what I thought of the place. To be perfectly frank with you, I didn't know whether to lie and make her feel good, or tell the truth. After a few seconds I decided to tell the truth.

"Well," I said, "it's this way. I have the feeling you could use a few more things."

She smiled. "What sort of things, Mr. Scully?"

"You know. Some more furniture, or maybe a TV to keep you company in the evenings. You could get a portable for around a hundred dollars."

She pointed at all the books. "I have a great deal of company in the evenings."

"Well, that's true. But what I mean is, you don't seem to own very much."

"On the contrary, sir. I own a view of the sunset, the evening star, and a superb bed of tulips."

I groaned at this, because it seemed so far-out. Then Mrs. Woodfin stared into space, and I knew right away that she was going to quote something.

"'To see a world in a grain of sand
And a heaven in a wild flower,
Hold infinity in the palm of your hand
And eternity in an hour.'"

"William Shakespeare!" I said.

Mrs. Woodfin winked at me. "Wrong," she said. "William Blake."

We started to laugh then. I don't know why, but suddenly everything seemed funny and great and not far-out at all. Mrs. Woodfin might have been eighty years old but she laughed like a kid, and this tickled me so much that I just kept on laughing with her. Then she settled back in the rocker. Her eyes, as I have said before, were this very bright blue—which made her hair look all the whiter. And her skin was very smooth. Hardly wrinkled at all.

"When I was a little girl," she said, "we had a country place in Surrey—a Georgian estate with several hundred acres. It had been in my mother's family for years, so every summer we would pack our things and make the annual pilgrimage. I rather liked this change of scene, but my brother Osbert—Bertie, we called him—loathed it. You would have liked Bertie, Mr. Scully. He was a nonconformist from the age of five, when he decorated his room with garlands and held what he chose to call The Rites Of Spring. All the servants were forced to attend, and I'm sure they felt embarrassed dancing around the nursery with bunches of flowers. At ten, Bertie was a philosopher. At twelve, a mystic. Well, it was the summer of his fourteenth birthday, and we had no sooner arrived at Windmere—as the estate was called—when Bertie announced that he was through with worldly pleasures. He had been studying Buddhism and had come to the conclusion that the only way to find enlightenment was to renounce luxury. He thereupon gave me all his possessions, including the pony he had gotten for his birthday, kissed our parents good-bye, and moved into the potting shed."

"What's a potting shed?" I asked.

Mrs. Woodfin poured herself some sherry. "A little building where one pots plants. So, there was Bertie living in the potting shed, and there were the rest of us living in the house. At first my parents thought it was just a phase. After all, they had already seen him through Christianity and Judaism. And so they sent him encouraging little notes and had Soames, our butler, take him meals on a tray. But after two weeks they became alarmed. Bertie had not only shaved his head to look like a Buddhist monk, but had taken to wearing a burlap sack that smelled strongly of manure. His plan was to achieve enlightenment through meditation, and he would begin meditating every day at dawn, sitting cross-legged among the pots and trowels. I must say this made me angry, because I missed his company. 'Bertie,' I would call at the door of the shed, 'do come out. I've no one to play with.' But Bertie would just nod enigmatically—his mind upon the Buddha's four noble truths. He stayed in the potting shed all summer."

"Man," I said. "That's wild."

"I thought so myself," said Mrs. Woodfin, "because Bertie was a very spoiled boy. He had been given every luxury in the world. I never thought he would stick it out."

"And then what happened?"

"He continued to study Buddhism. Then, five years later, he went to Japan and joined a Zen Buddhist monastery. I visited him there once, and he was the happiest person I had ever seen."

This really surprised me. "You're kidding."

"I'm not."

I tried to imagine what a monastery was like. It would probably be very peaceful. "Is he still there?" I asked.

"Oh, yes. I hear from him occasionally, and Bertie is now the oldest monk in Kyoto. But very lively. The Zen people are quite chipper, you know."

We grinned at each other, and I thought how much it was like Mrs. Woodfin to have a brother who was a real Buddhist. Not just some kind of a nut, but a guy who practised what he preached. Then I had some more tea, and a sandwich, and by the time I left her house I was in a very good mood. In addition to which, she had loaned me a book on Blake.

I walked home slowly so I could think about Mrs. Woodfin and her brother Bertie, and the more I thought about her the more I realized how much I liked her. It was even possible that she had a point about owning the evening star. I myself am very interested in stars, because they show you how vast and beautiful the universe is. I even tried to save up for a telescope once. But I couldn't get it because it was too expensive. I don't know. A part of me dug Mrs. Woodfin, and the other part was just lonely. The lonely part was familiar to me, but the part that dug her was like an amnesia victim who was stumbling around trying to remember his name. I know that doesn't make much sense, but it's what I mean.

I thought about this when I got home, and I was thinking of it during dinner when my mother said, "I read the most fabulous thing in *House Beautiful* today."

My father was staring at his second martini. "What's that?" he asked.

"Stoves will soon be obsolete," said my mother. "Totally obsolete. Instead, they're going to hang the range in the middle of the kitchen and call it a Cooking Island."

"How do you get to it—by boat?" my father said. I laughed at this but my mother didn't, because you could see that she wanted this Cooking Island very badly. Last week it had been a sprinkler for the lawn that had feet and walked by itself, and the week before that it had been an electric back massager from Abercrombie & Fitch. I looked at my father, and he didn't look despairing like he sometimes does, but just resigned. And I had this vision of him making payments on Cooking Islands for the rest of his life. Then one day he would die, and since he didn't have any friends there would be no one to come to the funeral but me and my mother and all our appliances. I could just see the TV set and the vacuum cleaner and the washing machine sitting in the funeral parlor trying to cry, but unable to because they didn't have feelings.

This thought upset me so much that I got up from the table and went to my room without having dessert. It was only eight-fifteen, but I got into bed anyway. Orson was already asleep on the bed with his paws over his eyes. He always sleeps that way. It must be to keep out the light or something. I started to read Mrs. Woodfin's book on Blake, who was a pretty interesting guy it turned out, but after a few chapters my mind began to wander. All I could really think of was what Bertie would have said about that Cooking Island.

13 I went to Mrs. Woodfin's every day after that, and here is the way it worked. On Mondays I would tell my mother that I was rehearsing for the Dramatics Club, and on Tuesdays I would tell her I was rehearsing for the Glee Club. On Wednesdays I explained that I had to attend the French Club, and on Thursdays I said that the Chess Club was meeting. This only left Fridays for which I invented a club called The Foreign Affairs Discussion Group.

I had taken care of Saturdays by saying that I had baseball practice, so all in all, my mother was quite shook up. She couldn't get over how normal I had become and kept telling me how pleased she was. She even bought me a baseball mitt. This was rather sad, of course, but I just couldn't tell her that I was seeing the old lady who had made me drunk that time. Not that I had had a drink since. I just drank tea and let Mrs. Woodfin have the sherry.

But the point is, I had something to look forward to now. And if Mrs. Woodfin minded my coming over so much, she didn't let on. She probably knew a lot more interesting people than me, but she still acted like she enjoyed my company. Each day she would meet me at the front door and make my tea while I sat at the kitchen table—and the funny thing was that I was getting to like tea very much. Then we would talk about things, and some of our conversations were quite unusual. We talked about the war in Vietnam, which she was against too, and television and movies, and LSD, and there wasn't a single subject that she wasn't an expert on. You would think that somebody eighty years old would never have heard of LSD, but she said that the Mexican Indians had been using similar stuff for years—in their ceremonies and everything. She also knew about discothéques and pop art and Happenings, and even knew what the word "camp" meant. I myself had never known what it meant until I read about it in *Life* magazine.

The interesting part was that Mrs. Woodfin was so broad-minded. Here she was, raised in the Victorian times, and still being able to accept things like sex and marijuana and space-travel. And even though she didn't personally dig some of these things, she wasn't against them. "To each his own, Mr. Scully," she would say to me. "To each his own." One day I had asked her how she could be so tolerant about everything, and she had said it was because she had lived a very long time and had come to realize that while styles of living changed, human beings didn't. And that human beings were basically good. I guess the only two things that Mrs. Woodfin disliked were war and con-formity. As for the rest, she was open to suggestion.

To be perfectly frank with you, I hadn't had a real conver-sation with anyone in five years. So it was really nice to have someone to talk to. Not just anybody, but a special person who knew how to listen and who respected your ideas. And also, I was starting to feel at home in her house. I couldn't under-stand how it had seemed so unattractive at first because now it seemed great. To begin with, it was great not to have a TV shouting at you every minute. And secondly, it was great to be in a place that was so messy that you could relax. Nobody at my house can use a glass without my mother washing it, and everywhere you look there are four million cans of Ajax Double

Bleach Cleanser. But Mrs. Woodfin's messiness had a point to it, because once you got over the shock, it was rather homey. And also, we both liked sandwiches. I have this habit of clipping sandwich recipes from ladies' magazines, which irritates my mother, but which I do simply because I love sandwiches. And so did Mrs. Woodfin. She never had much food in the house, so every day I would stop off at the A&P to get some sandwich things and the little cigars she liked, and together we made some fantastic concoctions: red caviar and cream cheese on white, sardine and onion on rye, and cucumber and mayonnaise on very thin whole wheat.

By now you will understand that Mrs. Woodfin had become my friend. Which is the important part of this story. She wasn't just an acquaintance or an old lady anymore, but a complete friend. The kind of person you could be with when you had a terrible cold, or the kind of person who wouldn't go to pieces if your fly came unzipped. And the fact of having a friend made me remember the only other friend I had had—a kid called Billy Marks.

Billy Marks and I had been around ten years old when we met, and it was love at first sight because we were both funny-looking and shy and lousy in school. We had been friends for six months, and they were about the best months of my life because Billy would take me home with him every afternoon. His family was poor, but I hadn't really noticed because they were all such great people. There were five kids, and Billy's parents who were on relief, and his grandmother who had come to live with them recently. And in spite of money troubles, there was always something good to eat at their house and everybody laughed a lot. What I mean is, these people really loved each other and weren't embarrassed to hug each other in front of you. They even loved me, in a way, and I guess that's what got me. What also got me was Billy Marks himself, because he was a very sensitive little kid. At the time I knew him, he was hipped on frogs, and there must have been a hundred of them in a tank in his room. He caught them in a creek near the house, and they were always dying. But no matter which one of them died, even if it was the worst-looking frog you ever saw, he would have a complete funeral for it. With flowers and prayers and everything. I must have attended fifty funerals in the time I knew Billy Marks, and I really enjoyed them.

But then I brought Billy home to supper one night, and the whole friendship collapsed because of my mother. I had never thought about Billy being poor or badly dressed or anything like that, but the minute I brought him in the house my mother acted like I had brought in a zebra. She was very polite, but the trouble is she was too polite. And she would say these embarrassing things to Billy at the dinner table like, "The *small* fork is for salad, dear," or "Would you like me to cut your meat for you?" Which made it seem like Billy was uncouth or something.

Well, the whole evening was like that, and when I walked Billy to the bus he said that it would probably be better if we weren't friends anymore. This was such a terrible thing for him to say that I couldn't believe it. "But why?" I said. "What's wrong?" He gave me this funny look and said, "What's wrong? Nothing but the world, that's all." It had taken me a long time to understand what he meant, but the awful thing was that Billy and I were never close again. We saw each other in school every day, but it wasn't the same.

I had missed Billy Marks ever since. I even dreamed about him once after he and his family moved to Brooklyn. But now that I knew Mrs. Woodfin, Billy's memory didn't seem so painful. I would remember how funny-looking he had been and how serious he was about his frogs, and how he had this habit of whistling when he was trying to concentrate. But you know- even though he had only been ten, Billy Marks understood a great deal about life.

14 "It all began on a Monday in April," said Mrs. Woodfin. "I was on my way to the theater, and my mind was preoccupied because I had a rehearsal for *Twelfth Night* that afternoon."

"How old were you?" I asked.

"Twenty-one, Mr. Scully, and so well-known that people stared at me in the street. The traffic was heavy that day, but I took little notice of it because I was going over my lines. Well, I was just crossing Drury Lane, reciting Viola's big speech in the second act, when a carriage thundered down on me. I stood absolutely frozen and would have been killed had not a hand reached out and pulled me roughly to the curb. I looked up to see who had rescued me—and found myself gazing into the eyes of the handsomest young man I had ever seen."

"Gee," I said. "What a great beginning."

"It was indeed, though at the time I was too shaken to think so. I was on the verge of fainting, so the young man helped me into a tearoom and sat me down at a table. He dampened his handkerchief in a glass of water and pressed it to my temples. 'You ought to watch where you're going,' he said sternly. When I recovered myself, I saw that this handsome stranger did not recognize me. I might have been the toast of the London stage, but to him I was only a silly girl who had almost got run over."

"Didn't that bug you? Not being recognized, I mean."

"On the contrary, Mr. Scully, it rather fascinated me. The young man's name was Peter, and he was glorious to behold: tall, with strong features and a head of curly black hair. He immediately announced that he was a poet, and I sensed some vanity in the statement because his clothes were threadbare. 'Have you been published?' I inquired. 'Not yet,' he said, 'but I shall be.' Quite suddenly I decided not to reveal myself to him. Instead, I said that I was a shop-girl named Sarah Williams who lived in Soho."

"Why?" I asked.

"A lark," sighed Mrs. Woodfin. "Simply a lark."

It was a rainy day, and I was stretched out on the floor by the fireplace. For some reason the lights weren't working, and the room was sort of dim. Mrs. Woodfin was sitting in the rocker. I looked at her and thought how pretty she must have been at twenty-one. "What happened then?"

"We left the tearoom and went for a stroll along the Thames. Peter did all of the talking. He had come to London without a penny in his pocket and was living over a stable; taking odd jobs during the day and writing poems at night. The publishers were afraid of his work because it was unconventional. And yet, he assured me, he would be a very great poet one day."

"Did you ever get to your rehearsal?"

Mrs. Woodfin laughed. "I did not. Before I knew it, it was five o'clock—and Peter was still talking. He asked if he might see me again, and so I agreed to meet him the following afternoon. And all the way home I thought what a splendid lark it was—something to tell my friends at the theater. Alas, Mr. Scully, I was soon to change my mind. We met in front of the tearoom every day after that, and by the end of two weeks we were hopelessly in love. What I had thought was vanity in Peter was simply bravado. Beneath the surface he was very innocent.

And thoroughly romantic. A country boy, he would wake in the middle of the night, throw on his clothes, rush out into the streets to drink the atmosphere of the city, and then rush back again to write by moonlight. He wanted to know it all—the noise, the bustle, the crowds—and if he had to write his poems on butcher paper, he did not feel demeaned. All life was exciting to him, and I expect it was this ingenuousness that won my heart. But I was now in a predicament, for Peter had fallen in love with a shop-girl, not a famous actress. He was secure with Sarah Williams, but Orpha Jennings would have terrified him. He was working class, you see, while my family was titled and wealthy. I decided that I would never tell him the truth."

"But how did you keep it from him?"

"It wasn't easy, I assure you. I told him that my father disapproved of my seeing young men, and that my employer at the dress shop was very strict. Oh, I invented a thousand excuses to keep him from taking me home or seeing where I really worked. And all the while, I knew that I was heading for disaster."

I sat up. "There's something I don't get. How come he hadn't seen you on the stage?"

"Because he was too poor to attend the theater," Mrs. Woodfin explained. "He was so poor that he could not even take me to a restaurant. We spent most of our time walking. I had never really looked at the city before, but now, with Peter, all London became beautiful. Then the day arrived when he turned to me on the street and said, 'When will you marry me, Sarah?' It was more of a statement than a question, and his face was very grave as he said it; the face of a somber, trusting child. I knew then that we would have to part. The following afternoon I did not appear at the teashop."

For some reason this shook me up. "But that's terrible!" I said. "Didn't you really love him?"

"I adored him, Mr. Scully. But how could I justify all those lies? Peter was good and innocent and kind—and I had deceived him. A week later I opened in *Twelfth Night*, and never had a role seemed more poignant to me. As you will remember, Viola is in love with a man who does not know her identity. I played her with all my heart that night, and after the curtain calls I went back to my dressing room and wept. Then the door opened, and Peter was standing there—a bunch of violets in his hand. He had known about me all along, you see. All along."

It was raining harder now, and the windows were getting steamed up. Mrs. Woodfin seemed to have forgotten I was there, because she was gazing at the rain with this distant look on her face. After a while she went on.

"I married Peter Woodfin soon afterwards, Mr. Scully, and we had two years of perfect happiness."

"And then what happened?"

"He died of consumption," she said.

"Gee. I'm sorry ..."

"You mustn't be. We had greater joy in those two years than most people have in a lifetime. I took a vacation from the theater, we traveled on the continent, and Peter's first poems were published. He never believed that he was dying. He made wonderful plans—even to the end."

"Gee," I said. "How sad."

"It was after Peter's death that I gave up the theater. I had known perfect happiness with him; and compared to that happiness, fame, ambition, and glory were meaningless. Peter, you see, had taught me that the only happiness is love."

"Where is he buried?" I asked. I didn't want to upset her or anything, but I wanted to know.

"In Shropshire," said Mrs. Woodfin. Her voice was very quiet. "A lovely cemetery with a view of rolling hills. When they lowered him into the ground, I placed two roses on the casket. A red one for him, a white for me."

Mrs. Woodfin went on talking, but I didn't hear much of what she said because all of a sudden I was in this place called Shropshire, England, watching Peter being lowered into the ground. It was a rainy day, and there weren't many people there. Just me and Mrs. Woodfin, and maybe Peter's parents. And I thought how awful it must be to die young when you had been a poet and everything, and in love.

And then I guess my imagination sort of got away from me, because it seemed that I was bending down and putting my own rose on Peter Woodfin's grave. A yellow one. For Albert.

15 If I could write like Shakespeare or somebody, I would be filling this story with exciting events—like having my father rob the insurance company, or having my mother drown in the bathtub while reading *House Beautiful*. But the truth of the matter is that this story is biographical, which is a limited thing because it means that you have to be honest. If all this honesty weren't required, I would present myself in a better light. But it isn't possible. I've got to tell you what really happened, and what really happened wasn't thrilling. I didn't murder that Psychologist I told you about or suddenly get an A in Algebra. And I didn't run away to New Zealand. What happened was this:

1. I stopped thinking about Herbie Steiner so much. How popular he was and everything.
2. I stopped taking so many baths.
3. I planted more flowers in the back yard.
4. I told Mrs. Woodfin how I wanted to work on a tugboat.

I admit that these events aren't exactly earth-shattering, but they were important to me because all of a sudden I was starting to feel relaxed. If you are a tense person, being relaxed is almost like being drunk. You get sort of gay and stop caring about things. It didn't seem to matter so much that I was still failing in school, and it didn't seem to matter that my parents were still arguing about me. These arguments had been going on since I was in the first grade: Was I retarded? Why couldn't I get better marks? What was going to become of me? Why couldn't I be like other kids? Why didn't I have any friends? Well, I had been listening to these arguments for years and feeling guilty about them. You know. As if everything in the universe was my fault. But now it was occurring to me that maybe I wasn't such a moron as my mother said. Don't get me wrong. I didn't blame her for thinking I was a moron, because from her point of view she was right. But on the other hand, it was occurring to me that from another point of view she might be wrong..

You see, Mrs. Woodfin didn't think I was a moron at all. To her, I was a very interesting person. If she had been putting me on, I would have known it. But she wasn't. She really thought I was OK, and the fact that she thought this made me feel sort of different. I mean, all of a sudden I didn't feel so embarrassed about my gardening. Or my recipe collection. Or the fact that I liked Shakespeare. I just started to accept these things, and it occurred to me that if Thoreau could have a different drummer, maybe I could too. I know this doesn't make much sense, but I kept wondering if there wasn't a drummer for me somewhere. A kind of beautiful person who was beating a drum with my name on it. A kind of poet maybe, like Peter, who was strolling through the world beating this very slow uneven beat that no one could hear but me.

I don't know. All of this is hard to explain—but it was like I was seeing myself through Mrs. Woodfin's eyes or something. In the beginning I had been embarrassed when she would pay me compliments about how attractive I was, or what a good mind I had. But now I just let her say these things, and a part of me believed her because she was the most honest person I had ever met. What I am trying to say is, Mrs. Woodfin would have been burned at the stake rather than tell a lie. She practised what she preached too, in the sense that she had given up worldly things just like her brother Bertie. And you could see that she really got pleasure from the simple things in life: her measly tulips, her books, her view. I had always thought she was poor, so I was very surprised when she told me that she had some money saved but that she was leaving it to Bertie's monastery in Japan. Which made her way of life pretty noble when you thought about it. Last of all, she was a completely "different" person and couldn't have cared less what people thought about her. Here was the whole world rushing around in miniskirts and trying to be fashionable—and there was Mrs. Woodfin hobbling through her house in a long velvet dress simply because she had worn it once in a play called *Hedda Gabler* and was fond of it. It was incredible how much she was like Thoreau, and sometimes I found myself wishing that old Henry could come back to life and meet her. I could just see them sitting at the kitchen table talking about Nature and the pencil business and having a ball.

I had been re-reading *Hamlet* lately and thinking how much I used to be like him. In the sense that I had been such a worrier. Hamlet is about the biggest worrier in literature, and there are times when you get annoyed with him because no sooner does he decide to do something than it occurs to him that it might not be the *right* thing, so he winds up doing nothing. Which is very irritating, considering how bright he is basically. Anyway, I had come across a very good quotation in *Hamlet* that went like this:

... blest are those whose blood and judgement are so well commingled that they are not a pipe for fortune's finger to sound what stop she please.

What Shakespeare is trying to say here is that if you balance your feelings and your logic, life won't bug you. I had thought about this for days because *I* had been a pipe that fortune had been playing on like crazy. At school. At home. At "The Tramp's Ball." Everywhere. And I hadn't even known it. That's the incredible thing—I hadn't known it at all.

16

Mrs. Woodfin and I were having sardine and onion sandwiches, and I was telling her my theories on air pollution.

"Here's the problem," I said. "Everybody thinks that the atmosphere will always be breathable—but it won't. One day it will get so polluted that we won't be able to fix it, and then the whole planet will suffocate to death. I probably won't be around when that happens, but it worries me anyway. The point is, here's Nature trying to fill the world with fresh air, and there's industry polluting it just to make money. I mean, you'd think that having polluted everything else, they'd leave the air alone, wouldn't you?"

"You would indeed," said Mrs. Woodfin.

"And here's another thing. I've only lived in this development for a couple of years, but when I moved in there were some fields around here. You know. Open spaces with trees in them. Well, not anymore. Everywhere you turn they are either putting up an industrial park or a housing development, and you could break your neck just looking for a tree. It just kills me the way these contractors come in with their bulldozers and root up the land and the trees. If they would put the trees back, it might be OK. But they don't. They cut them up."

"I know," said Mrs. Woodfin.

"Which is why I am so interested in New Zealand," I said.

"New Zealand is about the most unspoiled country in the world—and one of the least populated. They only have twenty-three people to every square mile, which is really the height of privacy. And on top of that, they have this fantastic scenery: volcanoes, beaches, glaciers, forests, plains. All that scenery, and only twenty-three people to every mile. It seems to me that a person could really be peaceful in New Zealand. I mean, you wouldn't have to compete or anything. You could just do something simple, like being a sheep farmer, and nobody would criticize you for it."

Mrs. Woodfin wasn't very talkative today, but I didn't mind because I had so much to say myself. I was really wound up.

"Take Cape Cod. My parents and I went there twice for a summer vacation, and the first time it was great. There was just this little town with an inn, and then miles of open space leading to the ocean. Well, that didn't last either. We went back to this town three years later and everywhere you looked there was either a hot dog stand or an antique shop or a Dairy Queen."

I took a bite of my sandwich and thought about Cape Cod. I had loved it there because it was the first time I had ever seen the ocean, and I had spent whole days just walking on the beach. I didn't know how to swim, but it hadn't mattered because the ocean was so big and clean and beautiful to watch. I had walked along the beach pretending to be Balboa or Columbus or somebody, and it had seemed like there was nobody else in the world but me. But after we had been there twice, we stopped going because my father couldn't afford it anymore. This had made me feel bad, because even though he didn't say much about it, you could tell that he had loved it too. I mean, he had bought goggles and fins and everything, for skin diving. Now he has this little vinyl pool that he sets up in the yard every summer, and I don't think there is any sight more pathetic than my father in his swimming trunks sitting in this tiny pool from Korvette's. It really depresses me.

"Listen," I said to Mrs. Woodfin. "Do you think that the people in New Zealand smoke and drink and take drugs and everything?"

"I don't know, Mr. Scully. Why do you ask?"

"Oh, I don't know. I was just hoping that they didn't. I mean, sometimes it seems to me that every person in the human race is hung up on something. The kids are hung up on drugs, and their parents are hung up on drinking and cigarettes, and everybody in the world seems to be getting cancer. I don't know. I was just hoping that it might be different in New Zealand."

Mrs. Woodfin reached over and smoothed the hair off my forehead. It was a warm day and I was sort of sweating.

"I am sure that it is different in New Zealand," she said.

And then I got this idea.

"Man!" I said. "I've got it. Why don't you and I take a little trip somewhere? My summer vacation is coming up, and while I'll have to be tutored, we might just take a day off and go to New York. We could go to the Natural History Museum and the Cloisters and maybe even take the boat ride around Manhattan. That boat ride is great. Listen, it really would be possible. I've got some Christmas money saved and I could pay for us both."

Mrs. Woodfin looked so funny when I said this that I thought I had offended her. But then she said,

"Mr. Scully, that is the most beautiful invitation I've ever had."

She was looking sort of tired, which I hadn't noticed before.

"Do you feel all right?" I asked.

She poured a glass of sherry and began to sip it. "It's just a headache. I've been reading too much, I suppose. Would you be good enough to get me some aspirin from the medicine chest?"

"Sure," I said.

I went into her bathroom and started rummaging around in the medicine chest. And suddenly I felt very let down, because I realized that we couldn't go to New York after all. Not with her being crippled and everything. The thing that was the matter with her was arthritis, and now she was getting headaches. It was too bad, because I really would have liked going with her.

I found the aspirin and brought them back to the kitchen. Mrs. Woodfin took one and washed it down with sherry.

"Would you like me to rub your neck?" I asked. "Sometimes that helps."

"No, no, Mr. Scully. I'll be right as rain in a moment. Tell me, how are you doing in school?"

I started to make another sandwich. "Lousy," I sighed. "Absolutely lousy. You wouldn't believe how bad I'm doing."

"Why do you suppose that is?"

She was staring at me like she wanted a real answer. Which was the thing about Mrs. Woodfin—she always made you think.

"Do you know what it is?" I said suddenly. "It's because nothing I'm studying is connected to anything. That's what it is! Take Algebra. What is it supposed to do for you? You couldn't balance a checkbook with Algebra or add up a grocery list or anything. Or take Latin. Why should I learn to speak Latin when I live in New Jersey? Nothing's *connected*."

Well the minute I said that, I got excited, because I felt like I had hit on something.

"Do you know what kids should study?" I said. "How to stop wars, that's what they should study. And how to love people. And how not to be confused about sex. Here we are studying Algebra and Latin, when the real problems in life are love and sex and war. And loneliness! Man, if any teacher would teach you what to do about loneliness, I'd give him a million bucks. Why does everybody go to psychiatrists? Because they're lonely, that's why. I mean, it's really pathetic when you have to *pay* somebody to listen to your troubles. Then there are those radio programs where you call the announcer on the phone and talk to him. Have you ever listened to them? People have nothing to say to those announcers, absolutely nothing. They just call up and say what a great show it is and how they like the announcer—and all because they're lonely. They can't talk to their wives and kids, so they call a million announcers.

I was so excited that I took a slug of Mrs. Woodfin's sherry before I knew what I was doing. "And being a hippie isn't the answer, either. I went to Greenwich Village once, and I can tell you from experience that they're just as confused as everybody else. 'Don't trust anyone over thirty' they say. Boy, what a cop-out. Albert Einstein was the most brilliant person in the whole world, and he was way over thirty."

By now I was out of breath, so I stopped for a minute.

"I guess all this sounds pretty wild."

Mrs. Woodfin leaned across the table and put her hand on my shoulder. "Mr. Scully," she said, "I have the distinct feeling that you are going to be all right."

I wasn't sure what she meant by that, but I didn't have a chance to ask because she said she wanted to rest. Her headache must have been worse, so I helped her into the bedroom and she lay down. I asked if she wanted me to leave, but she said, "No, my dear. Read to me."

I went into the other room and looked at her books. Shakespeare, Blake, Donne, Chekov, Virginia Woolf, Tolstoy, Flaubert. Suddenly it occurred to me that this was the first time

I had ever been alone in this room, so I started looking around at things. You can never really look at a person's things when they are watching you, but when you're alone it's different. For example, there was a bird's nest on the mantle that I had never noticed before, and in it were two little eggs. Empty, of course. Then there were some stones on the windowsill that looked like they had come from the seashore, and an ashtray that said Welcome To Atlantic City. I also noticed a little white elephant with a broken trunk and a jar of rose petals. But the strangest thing was this old wooden cigarette box that looked like some kid had made it. I opened the lid and inside was a card that said, "For Mrs. Woodfin from her loving ..." I couldn't make out the last word. Then I started to feel guilty about looking at all these things, so I chose a book that Mrs. Woodfin had quoted from once and took it back to the bedroom. It was called *Letters To A Young Poet*. By Rilke.

I sat down and opened the book in the middle and started to read aloud.

"'Here, where an immense country lies about me, over which the winds pass coming from the seas, here I feel that no human being anywhere can answer for you those questions and feelings that deep within them have a life of their own; for even the best err in words when they are meant to mean most delicate and almost inexpressible things. But I believe nevertheless that you will not have to remain without a solution if you will attach yourself to objects that are similar to those from which my eyes now draw refreshment. If you will cling to Nature, to the simple in Nature, to the little things that hardly anyone sees, and that can so unexpectedly become big and beyond measuring; if you have this love of inconsiderable things and seek quite humbly, as a ministrant, to win the confidence of what seems poor: then everything will become easier, more coherent and somehow more conciliatory for you, not in your intellect, perhaps, which lags behind astonished, but in your inmost consciousness, waking and cognizance.'"

I glanced at Mrs. Woodfin and she was smiling at me. Her eyes looked very blue.

"'You are so young, so before all beginning, and I want to beg you, as much as I can, dear sir, to be patient towards all that is unsolved in your heart and to try to love the *questions themselves* like locked rooms and like books that are written in a very foreign tongue. Do not now seek the answers, that cannot be given you because you would not be able to live them. And the point is, to live everything ...'"

"You know," I said, staring at the book, "I sort of dig this guy. How do you pronounce his name? Rilkee or Rilkuh?"

But Mrs. Woodfin had fallen asleep.

17 It was about three nights later, and I was sitting at the desk with my History book. My parents were watching TV in the living room, and Orson was in the closet again. Waiting for that mouse.

Don't get the impression that I was *studying* my History book, because I wasn't. As a matter of fact, I had almost decided to give up studying for the rest of my life. You see, the minute I had made that speech to Mrs. Woodfin about school not being connected to anything, I had had a big revelation. Which was this: I didn't care about school. I had spent my whole life trying to care about it when I didn't. And why had I tried to? Because everybody else did. Which made no sense. I mean, there was war in the world, but did that make war right? And millions of kids were taking LSD and going insane, but was it right just because they did it? Therefore what was so hot about school? Nothing—except that you were forced to go.

The way I had described my school to Mrs. Woodfin was absolutely true. They didn't teach you a single thing that was important. They didn't even have Sex Education, which some schools do nowadays starting from the first grade. I really could have used some Sex Education in the first grade. Now, of course, it was too late. But when I was in the first grade I could have used it very badly because this girl named Carol Meister, who lived next door, was always asking me to play doctor with her. And like a fool I had played once and gotten into terrible trouble with her father.

I thought about these things, and then I got up from the desk and dropped my History book in the wastebasket. "Ashes to ashes and dust to dust," I said.

At that very moment my mother walked in. She never knocks.

"Albert?" she said. "Sweetheart? What are you doing?"

I started to fish around in the wastebasket like crazy. "I dropped a book in here," I said.

My mother sat down on the bed and lit a cigarette. "Sit down, sweetheart. I want to talk to you."

So I sat down next to her, and I could see that something was up because she was acting very friendly.

"Darling?" she said. "Yes, Mom?"

"You know that Mother loves you, don't you?"

"Sure," I said.

"And Daddy, too? You must know how much Daddy loves you."

I was starting to feel a little embarrassed. "Well, sure."

"There isn't a thing in this world that Mother and Daddy wouldn't do for you, Albert. You must know that."

"I *do*," I said. "Gee whiz …"

"If I get irritable with you sometimes, it's only because I'm worried," she went on. "You see, Daddy and I have been doing some talking, and while we are terribly excited about all your extracurricular activities, we are still very worried about your grades."

This, by the way, wasn't true. Because my father didn't care at all.

"I'm sorry," I said.

She put her arm around my shoulder. "Darling, being sorry

is just not the answer. You'll have to be tutored all summer, and by next year you should be thinking about college. Don't you care about college?"

"No," I said.

My mother pretended not to hear this. Which is an interesting device she has. You could write a whole book on it.

"It's not that I mind paying for this tutoring, but you've got to do your part, too. You see, Albert, while I'm not complaining, I've sacrificed a great many things for you."

"I know," I said.

"You've always had the best, but in order to give you the best, I've had to go without a great many things I would have liked. A great many things, I assure you."

By now my mother was starting to lose her cool. Her voice wasn't so sweet anymore and she had dropped an ash on the carpet. And yet it was like she was alone in the room. She wasn't really noticing me.

"Do you think I've done all this for myself?" she said, staring out the window. "From the day you were born, I've been trying to give you things I never had. Dancing lessons. Piano lessons. Good clothes. And a lovely home where you could bring your friends. Do any of your friends have a lovelier home than this? Of course they don't. We're not millionaires, but you've had every luxury we could afford. Air conditioning, television ..."

"I don't want air conditioning," I said. But she didn't hear me, because she had gotten up and was walking around waving her cigarette like Bette Davis. For one crazy minute I wanted to ask her not to blow smoke in the room because of Orson. She is always blowing smoke around him, and I worry about his getting cancer.

"I have been saving for your college education from the day you were born, Albert. I've borrowed from the household money, taken part-time jobs, denied myself pleasures. Do you think I've done all that for myself? Do you?"

And then—Zap! Pow! Wham!—I saw it. The whole thing. She had been doing it for herself. All of it. The piano lessons, the clothes, everything. It was like I was a stock on Wall Street that she had invested in years ago, and now this stock wasn't paying off. This very expensive stock called Albert Scully was going bust—so she was furious.

This was such a tremendous thing to discover that I wanted to tell her about it right away. I didn't hate her or anything—I just wanted to tell her. So we could clear all these lies from the air and be honest with each other and maybe love each other again. What I wanted to say was, "Mom, Mom, listen to me. I know I'm a disappointment to you, but the reason I'm such a disappointment is that you don't see me. You're getting all upset over a person who doesn't exist. I'm never going to get into college or be a great man or make a lot of money. I'm just me, Albert ..." But I couldn't say this, because she was going a mile a minute.

"And that alcoholic in the next room!" she said. "Do you think I get any help from him? If it weren't for me, the three of us would have starved years ago. Do you think I've had such a wonderful life? Do you think I've had a single moment's happiness with that insurance salesman in there?"

And then I looked up and saw my father standing in the door.

"*The Man From UNCLE* is on TV," he said.

"I'm going out!" said my mother, pushing past him. "I'm getting in the car and just going out."

My father and I stood there looking at each other. And I felt terrible, because I knew he had heard the whole thing.

"*The Man from UNCLE* is on TV," he said again. Then he went back to the living room.

18 I guess that any person with an ounce of compassion would have tried to make my father feel better that night, but I didn't. Maybe it was because I was starting to see that the real trouble in our house was between my parents and didn't have much to do with me. Or maybe it was just callousness. I don't know. But things were moving so fast that I didn't have time to think about anyone but myself. That sounds awful, I know, but it's true. And the fact that it was June and exams were coming up didn't even seem to matter. Nothing mattered anymore except me and Mrs. Woodfin and this incredible friendship we had. It was like we were drifting far above the world in one of those old-fashioned balloons, drinking tea and looking down at the rest of humanity beating their brains out for no reason at all. And sometimes it seemed to me that Peter and Bertie were with us—Bertie wearing his monk's costume and being very cheerful, and Peter maybe reading his poems aloud. If you looked at it a certain way, we had become a kind of family: me, Mrs. Woodfin, Peter and Bertie.

By now Mrs. Woodfin had told me a lot more stories about Peter and Bertie and I really dug them. I mean, compared to Peter and Bertie, people like Herbie Steiner didn't seem to amount to much. Here was Bertie giving up everything for his religion, and there was Peter starving in London so he could write poems—and compared to them, a lot of people I used to admire suddenly seemed second-rate. Take Doris Day. It's hard to admit this, but I once had a very big crush on her which lasted a year. I had watched every one of her movies on TV, and I guess the reason I admired her so much was because she was such a regular person. I mean, Doris Day is so regular that nobody, not even the Communists, could be critical of her. And that's what had got me. But now I was beginning to see that when you came right down to it, Doris Day was a very boring person. The kind of person who would never be interested in Buddhism, and who wouldn't know a poem if she fell over it. That sounds mean, but all I am trying to say is that the Doris Day kind of person no longer attracted me. What attracted me now were people like Peter and Bertie and Mrs. Woodfin. Individuals.

I had always admired individuals, but I hadn't known it. That's the point. I hadn't known what I admired, and now I was starting to. Because here was a whole world full of people like Einstein and Thoreau and Peter and Bertie—and every one of them was listening to his own drummer. All of which brings me to my soul. I haven't mentioned my soul for quite a while, but I want to now because for the first time in my entire life it was feeling better. It still felt like a rhinoceros, but as though somebody had opened the door of its cage for a minute. To let it see what was outside.

Then there was my room. I don't know how other people feel about their rooms, but I had always felt depressed about mine because it just had a bed and a desk and a bureau in it—and that was all. Actually, it was sort of like a motel, even though my mother had put in plaid drapes and some automobile prints that she thought were "masculine." But now I had gotten sort of inspired about my room and had put up a big picture of Albert Einstein and a poster that said, "Make Love, Not War."

I had also taken my books out of the closet and made a book-case for them out of boards and bricks. Last of all, I had bought a little file drawer for my recipe collection and had framed some pictures of tugboats in dime store frames. My mother thought all this was crazy, of course, but I thought it was neat.

Well, it was Thursday afternoon, and I was on my way over to Mrs. Woodfin's. As usual. It was one of those summer days you get in New Jersey when the sky is all slate-colored and thundery and everybody's lawn looks very green. It was going to pour any minute, but I didn't care because I love walking in the rain. I love all kinds of weather. Even the humid kind you get in August. Anyway, I was strolling along the sidewalk thinking about Mrs. Woodfin, and suddenly it occurred to me how I *felt* about her. I had known for months that I liked her enormously, but all of a sudden I realized how I *felt* about her because a year ago I had had the exact same feeling in the Self-Service Coin-Operated Laundromat. To get off the point for a minute, I want to explain that if I ever decide to commit suicide, it will be in our local Self-Service Coin-Operated Laundromat. Man, is it depressing. The neon lights are so bright that it looks like an operating room, and all the drying machines look like iron lungs. You expect a head to stick out of one any minute. There are pink tiles on the floor and everything is very antiseptic, and people sit on these long plastic benches waiting for their laundry and looking stupified.

Anyhow, I had been in the Laundromat doing some laundry for my mother because our washing machine was broken, when I noticed this woman coming through the door. She was very thin and homely, with her hair in rollers, and she was dragging a little kid with her. Her laundry basket was full, and she was having trouble carrying it and also dragging the little kid. He must have been about three or something. Well, all of a sudden the little kid jerked away, and his mother dropped the basket. Shorts, brassieres, pajamas—all over the place. Which made her so mad that she started slapping the kid. And the more she slapped him, the louder he cried. She actually seemed to *enjoy* slapping him, which is the thing that amazed me. "You moron!" she said to him. "You stupid moron. Shut up!"

By now the kid was crying harder than ever, and I was feeling paralyzed—because the whole thing seemed so unfair. Here was this three-year-old who could hardly speak English, and there was his mother slapping him and calling him a moron. He wasn't even old enough to have any thoughts, and yet he was being called stupid just because he didn't like being dragged through a Self-Service Coin Operated Laundromat. This seemed so terrible that I wanted to rush over to that kid and grab him. What I mean is, I suddenly felt protective about him.

I realized that I couldn't grab this little kid away from his mother, and yet something had to be done because by now she was hitting him very hard. With her laundry all over the floor. So I just hurried up to her looking very urgent and said, "Lady, lady, this laundromat is on fire! No kidding. I just saw flames in the back room." Boy, did that do the trick. The woman went pale as a ghost and looked wildly around—as though she could really see the flames—and then she gave a little shriek and picked up her kid and ran. She didn't even bother about her laundry. She just rushed out to the parking lot and stood there, waiting for the fire.

I must have laughed for a whole week over that, yet at the same time I felt very pleased, because I had saved that little kid from being slapped black and blue. But the point is, the way I had felt about him was the way I felt about Mrs. Woodfin. Protective. Lately I had been noticing that I was always helping her in and out of chairs, and getting her things, and the interesting part is that I liked it. I certainly couldn't have acted this way with some high school girl, but Mrs. Woodfin was such a lady that I really enjoyed being nice to her. I was even nice to her in my dreams. I never used to dream much except for nightmares, but now I dreamed about Mrs. Woodfin all the time, and the funny thing was that in these dreams she was never crippled. Actually, she looked sort of beautiful in these dreams. And she would always be wearing a very elegant dress with jewelry. Sometimes we would be walking down a long street, and sometimes we would be sitting in a garden reading poems. But no matter where we were, there was nobody there but us, and I would be sort of looking after her. Once I even kissed her hand in a dream—which is not like me at all.

It had started to rain, and by the time I reached Mrs. Woodfin's house it was coming down cats and dogs. I knocked on the front door, but no one came so I went around to the back. I knocked there too, but no answer. Which seemed a little strange, but I figured she was napping. I tried the kitchen door, but it was locked, so I went back to the front and tried that one. Locked also. Then I started peering in the windows, but I couldn't see any sign of her. I wondered if she had gone out, but that didn't seem likely because she almost never did and certainly not in bad weather. With her cane and all. I just couldn't understand where she was, so finally I went next door and knocked there. After a few seconds a lady opened the door. I didn't know her because she was new in the neighborhood.

"Excuse me," I said. "Do you know where Mrs. Woodfin is?"

The lady had a dishtowel in her hand and she looked annoyed. "Who?"

"Mrs. Woodfin. The person who lives next door."

"Oh," she said. "You mean the old lady. They took her to the hospital last night."

"What?"

"She had a heart attack or something and phoned an ambulance. And I can tell you, the sirens made the worst racket I've ever heard. At three in the morning, yet."

"Are you sure?" I said.

"Of *course* I'm sure. It was three in the morning."

"Listen," I said, "listen! What hospital was it? I mean, where is she? Please! This is very important."

The lady gave me a funny look. "Memorial," she said. And then she closed the door.

I stood there in the rain and suddenly I was shaking all over, and the worst part was that I couldn't remember where Memorial Hospital was. I couldn't remember anything. The rain was coming down and I was shaking and I didn't know what to do. But then I came to my senses and ran to the bus stop, and after a few seconds a bus came along. I asked the driver where the hospital was, and he said it was on his route. So I paid my fare and sat down and I guess I was sort of praying, even though I don't believe in God. I just closed my eyes and prayed.

19 It took about thirty minutes to get to the hospital, and by the time I got there I was almost frantic. I just couldn't believe that anything had happened to Mrs. Woodfin, yet at the same time I knew it was true. She was gone and her house was locked up. She had had a heart attack. Then the woman at the main desk told me to go to the third floor, so I knew it was true. And all the way up in the elevator I was praying. I don't know what the prayers were. I just kept asking somebody, somewhere, to make things all right.

I got out at the third floor and hurried over to the nurse's desk. "Mrs. Orpha Woodfin," I said. "She's an actress."

"Room 340," said the nurse. "But you are not to stay more than ten minutes."

I started running down the hall looking for room 340, and the more I ran the more I could see what a terrible hospital it was. The walls needed painting, and the lights were dim, and there were all these carts with dirty dishes on them by the doors.

Then I found room 340 and went inside.

For a minute I couldn't see Mrs. Woodfin at all. There were just a lot of beds lined up with old ladies in them, and a couple of TV sets were playing very loud. It was terrible. Just a big drab room with curtains between the beds and no privacy. Then I saw her. She was near the window, and I almost didn't recognize her because she was wearing a hospital dress.

"Mrs. Woodfin!" I said. "Mrs. Woodfin, for God's sake …"

I ran over to her bed and I guess I must have looked very wild because she shook her finger at me.

"Not a *word*, Mr. Scully. Not a single word. Everything is under control."

Her voice was hoarse, and she looked awful. Yellow, sort of.

"But what happened?" I said. "I went to your house, and you were gone. What happened?"

"Mr. Scully, I am an old woman—and old women get heart attacks. There is nothing to be alarmed at. Becalm yourself, sir."

I looked around the room. One old lady was moaning, and another had tubes up her nose. It was awful.

"Mrs. Woodfin …"

"My dear young man, if you do not becalm yourself, I am going to send you packing. Haven't you ever seen a hospital before?"

"Well, yes," I said. "Once."

"Then what is all the clamor for? You look like Macbeth."

I tried to smile at this, but I was still very worried. "Are you going to be OK?" I asked. "Are they treating you OK?"

"Handsomely," said Mrs. Woodfin. "The nurses are jolly, and the food is superb. What more could one ask?"

The old lady in the next bed was moaning louder than ever. It really upset me.

"But all these sick people. It's so depressing. When can you come home?"

At that point a voice came over the loudspeaker. "Visiting hours are over," it said.

"You had better go, Mr. Scully."

I looked at her, and she looked very tired. Not like herself at all. "OK," I said, "but I'll be back tomorrow. Would you like some flowers?"

She nodded and closed her eyes, so there was nothing for me to do but leave. But the minute I got outside I went back to the nurse's desk.

"Listen," I said. "The lady in room 340. Mrs. Woodfin. Is she going to be all right?"

"I cannot give out that information," said the nurse.

"But I want to know about her heart and everything."

"You will have to speak to the doctor."

"OK. Where is he?"

"Dr. Kemp is off duty right now."

"For God's sake," I said. But then I realized that I wasn't going to get anything out of this nurse, so I took out my notebook and wrote down my name and phone number.

"Look, here's my name and phone number. If Mrs. Woodfin needs anything, would you call me? I'd really appreciate it."

"Are you a relative?" she asked.

"No," I said. "Just a friend. A very close friend."

I left the hospital and walked to the bus stop, and all the way home I felt terrible. Because here was Mrs. Woodfin in this dingy room full of old ladies and she didn't belong there at all. Not in a place where people had tubes up their nose. Mrs. Woodfin should have had a private room and a million nurses looking after her. People who cared. What if she got sick in the middle of the night and needed something? Who would come? Nobody. I bet they didn't even know she was famous.

I wondered how much it would cost to call Kyoto, Japan. That's where Bertie was, and he would want to do something right away. But then I realized that Bertie had been in Kyoto for so long that he probably spoke nothing but Japanese. So I just rode home on the bus with this empty feeling inside me, looking out at the rain.

To make things worse I got home very late, which annoyed my mother so much that she started scolding me. And then I guess I couldn't take any more, because I broke down and told her and my father the whole story. All of it. How I never had any extracurricular activities and how I had been seeing Mrs. Woodfin for months on the sly. And once I got going, I couldn't stop. I told them all about Mrs. Woodfin's career in the theater, and how her grandfather had been an Earl, and how they had a country house with servants. And then I told them about Peter and Bertie. I guess I must have been very upset, because they didn't even scold me. They just listened very quietly, and my father said how unfortunate it was that Mrs. Woodfin was sick. Then my mother asked if Mrs. Woodfin's grandfather had really been an Earl, and I said yes, and told her how Mrs. Woodfin had acted for Sarah Bernhardt, the most famous actress in the world. I just went on and on, and when I finished my mother patted my hand and said that she would bring me dinner on a tray. Which was such a nice thing for her to do that I was surprised.

I had dinner in my room that night, and by nine o'clock I had sort of calmed down. My father had said that not all heart attacks were serious, and that people in wards got excellent care. So I just calmed down about the whole thing and decided that I would bring Mrs. Woodfin some flowers the next day—to cheer her up until she could come home.

20 To tell you the truth, it had been a relief to tell my parents about Mrs. Woodfin. As though a weight had been taken off me or something. You see, for months I had been sneaking around the development like James Bond: getting off at different bus stops after school, and going home from Mrs. Woodfin's in a million roundabout ways. But now that my mother knew the situation, everything was better, and the strangest part of it was that she seemed interested. She talked about Mrs. Woodfin quite a lot now, and kept asking me about her grandfather the Earl and where they had lived in London. At first I couldn't figure this out. Mrs. Woodfin was, after all, quite a bit older than me and sort of unconventional. Then it dawned on me that my mother was impressed with her. Just like she is impressed with the Duchess of Windsor and Princess Margaret. My mother's family were grocers in Akron, Ohio, and I don't think she ever got over the disappointment. What I mean is, she is very impressed by class—anything that has money or a title attached to it. Which is why she is always reading *Vogue* and *Town And Country* and stuff like that.

On the other hand, you could see that my mother resented Mrs. Woodfin too—which is the ambivalent thing about her. She is always telling me to make friends, but the minute I make one, like that kid Billy Marks I told you about, she resents it. Not that I have ever had many friends, but a few years after

I knew Billy, I struck up an acquaintance with this older girl who worked in the local stationery store, and my mother was so critical of her that I had to let the whole thing go. As I said, she's ambivalent.

Anyhow, Mrs. Woodfin had been in the hospital for ten days and was much better. I wanted to visit her every day, of course, but I couldn't. These lousy exams were coming up, and my mother had made me promise that I would study for them and only see Mrs. Woodfin three times a week. Which wasn't much, but I tried to make up for it by bringing her flowers and some *National Geographics.*

One thing that still bothered me though, was that hospital. It was terribly noisy and the food was bad and there was never a nurse around when you wanted one. Look for a nurse and you would find them out at the desk, drinking coffee. Most of the work was done by these girls in striped uniforms who looked around twelve years old and giggled all the time. Then there were all those old ladies in Mrs. Woodfin's room. You never saw such terrible ladies. There was the one with tubes in her nose, and the one that moaned very loud, and one that called for somebody named Harold about fifty times a day. It was really depressing, and I couldn't imagine why Mrs. Woodfin didn't have a private room. I didn't want to say this to her, but it seemed to me that she should have used some of her savings for a private room instead of Bertie's monastery.

I guess the thing that got me was the impersonalness of the place, because there was nothing there to remind Mrs. Woodfin of home. Just a night table with Kleenex and a glass of water, and that was all. She didn't have any of her books and they had taken away her velvet dress, which made her look like a very different person. Mrs. Woodfin had always looked small, but now she looked kind of like a dwarf in that big hospital bed.

The amazing thing, though, was how cheerful she was being. I mean, if I had to lie in that dingy room with a lot of old ladies I would go off my rocker, but Mrs. Woodfin was terrific about it. She had made friends with every one of those old ladies and had told them all her stories about England and the theater. And the old ladies really seemed to dig this. They would sit up in their beds like a lot of frail birds and hang on to every word Mrs. Woodfin said. Sometimes she would recite plays for them, and once when I was there, two of them actually applauded. And even though she was in bed, Mrs. Woodfin had sort of taken a bow.

One afternoon one of these old ladies had pointed at me and said to Mrs. Woodfin, "Your grandson?" And Mrs. Woodfin had said, "My goodness, no. This is my dear friend Mr. Scully. A very brilliant young person who is interested in horticulture." Well, for some reason this had impressed the old ladies very much, and they had asked if they could meet me. So I had to go around to all the beds and shake hands with them, and I had never been more embarrassed in my life. On the other hand, the old ladies had seemed so glad to meet me that I got over my embarrassment in a few minutes, because I was beginning to see that they were kind of lonely.

I could hardly wait for Mrs. Woodfin to get well, and even though I was supposed to be studying for my exams, my mind was mainly on the things we would do when she got out of the hospital. She would have to take it easy, of course, but I figured that I could go over every day and take care of her. I might even cook for her too. So when you came right down to it, the situation was under control.

21 "It was the biggest joke of the twentieth century," I was saying. "Each test was three hours long, and I couldn't think of a single answer. I couldn't even do the essay questions."

I was sitting by Mrs. Woodfin's hospital bed, and sun was coming in the windows. Mrs. Woodfin was frowning.

"I find that highly suspicious," she said.

"Why?" I asked her.

"Because, Mr. Scully, you are a very intelligent person."

"But don't you remember what I said before? Nothing's *connected*."

She thumped on the blanket with her fist. "Doesn't matter, sir! We all have obligations in this world, and yours is to finish high school."

This was such a square thing for Mrs. Woodfin to say that I could hardly believe it. I looked around the room and all the old ladies were listening. I lowered my voice.

"I don't dig you, Mrs. Woodfin. I really don't."

She sighed. "My dear young man, can't you see that the only way to be unconventional is to fulfill your conventional obligations first? You must earn your right to be a nonconformist. Look at your friend Thoreau. He finished his education before he even thought of Walden Pond."

"OK," I said. "OK. What about Bertie?"

"Bertie had four years of preparatory school before he went to Japan."

I was getting a little depressed about this. I moved my chair closer to Mrs. Woodfin so the old ladies wouldn't hear me.

"Look, the only thing I want is to go to New Zealand or work on a tugboat. I know these are only dreams, but I thought you approved of them."

"Of course I approve of them! 'We are such stuff as dreams are made on, and our little life is rounded with a sleep.' *The Tempest.* Act Four."

Mrs. Woodfin lay back on the pillow and asked me to lower her bed. So I turned the handle that lowered it and then I filled her drinking glass with water.

"Dreams," she said, staring at the ceiling. "What dreams I had as a child ... At eight, I dreamed of being beautiful, and I became beautiful. At twelve, I dreamed of Africa. Safaris in the jungle heat, the roaring of beasts, a rhythm of drums. I went to Africa with my father. At sixteen, I dreamed of being the finest actress in the world. And so I played Ophelia, and the students drew my carriage through the streets of London, cheering ... Now I only dream of peace. But that, too, is beautiful. It is not the dream that matters, Mr. Scully, but the having of it."

"Louder!" said the old lady in the next bed. "I can't hear what you're saying."

"Later, dear," said Mrs. Woodfin.

"But you were going to recite for us," said the old lady. Her voice was very childish.

"And so I shall, my dear. At four this afternoon we shall have Oscar Wilde."

This seemed to shut the old lady up. She went back to reading her magazine.

"So what you are saying is that it's OK for me to have these dreams."

"OK?" said Mrs. Woodfin. "I would say that it was absolutely necessary. Dreams are the stuff of life, but they must be watched and guarded—as one would guard a splendid castle. You dream of going to New Zealand, Mr. Scully. You dream of sailing tugboats. Why shouldn't these things be possible? Henry David Thoreau had dreams, too. And the world thought he was mad."

Just then a nurse came over to us. "Mrs. Woodfin has to have her hypo," she said to me. "Please step outside."

So I went out to the hall while the nurse gave Mrs. Woodfin this hypo. There was some sort of tranquilizing medicine in it, and they gave it to her three or four times a day. I didn't want to watch because the needle was so long and everything.

After a few minutes I went back inside. Mrs. Woodfin's eyes were closed. It occurred to me that I was probably tiring her with so much talking.

"Mrs. Woodfin? Do you want me to leave or something?"

She opened her eyes. "No, no. What were we talking about?"

"Dreams," I said.

"I thought we were talking about Bertie ..."

"Well, not really."

She was staring out the window and one of her hands was fiddling with the blanket.

"Are you all right?" I asked.

"I'm fine, Mr. Scully. Just fine. And you will be, too."

I didn't know what she meant by this, but I decided not to ask because I could see that the hypo was affecting her. I straightened her night table and took some dead leaves off the flowers I had brought last week.

"Look," I said, "I'm going to let you get some rest now. But I'll be back tomorrow with some more *Geographics*. I'm also going to check on your house, just to see that everything's OK. Do you want me to water the garden?"

She didn't seem to be listening to me. Instead, she was looking out the window at these very high clouds that were sweeping the sky. It was a great day, with sun and wind and these very high clouds. You could see how much Mrs. Woodfin liked them, because she was gazing at them with this gentle look on her face.

"'Come,'" she said softly, " 'let's away to prison. We two alone will sing like birds in the cage: When thou dost ask me blessing, I'll kneel down and ask of thee forgiveness: so we'll live, and pray, and sing, and tell old tales, and laugh at gilded butterflies, and hear poor rogues talk of court news; and we'll talk with them too, who loses and who wins; who's in, who's out; and take upon us the mystery of things ...'"

She stopped, as though she couldn't remember any more.

"'As if we were God's spies...'" I finished.

"*King Lear*. Act Five."

And then Mrs. Woodfin did an amazing thing. A really amazing thing. She pulled my head down and kissed me.

22 Mrs. Woodfin was coming home in two days. The doctor had said so this morning, and I had gotten so excited that I had rushed out of the hospital without even saying good-bye. Because all of a sudden there was a lot to do. I had checked on her house a few times and watered the garden, but now I wanted to do something special. You see, for months Mrs. Woodfin had been great to me, and I had never done anything in return. I had gone over for tea every day, and she had listened to every one of my problems—yet it had never occurred to me to do anything for *her*. So now I decided that I would buy her something, and what I hit on was a rosebush. As a homecoming gift.

I went to a couple of greenhouses near Western Auto, and finally found the rosebush I wanted. It was really beautiful—a Peace rosebush with big yellow buds about to open. It cost two weeks' allowance, but it was worth every penny. I took it home to show my mother, and then I started over to Mrs. Woodfin's to plant it. About a block from my house, I saw Orson hiding under somebody's hedge, and I knew right away that the bluejays were after him again. Orson must be the only cat in America who gets chased by birds, but about three months ago he got into one of their nests, and they never forgot it. So now whenever they see him, they start dive-bombing him and screaming like crazy, and it really shakes him up. Sometimes he has to hide from them all day.

Orson watched me pass and didn't even flick a whisker. He was too cautious.

I got to Mrs. Woodfin's house and began walking around the back yard—looking for a spot to plant the roses. I wanted to put them someplace where she could see them from the window, but I also wanted them to get a lot of sun. Roses are very dependent on sun and moisture. Finally I found a good spot and dug a hole and filled it up with water from the hose. Then I lowered the bush in very carefully and covered it with earth. None of the gardening books will tell you this, but roses can sort of go into shock if you don't plant them right. I noticed that there was a little tag on one of the rose leaves that said "Peace," and I figured this would please Mrs. Woodfin. As though it were a message to everybody.

The rosebush looked so great that I suddenly decided to clean up the yard to go with it. So I gathered all the trash—garbage, old magazines, newspapers—and put it by the side of the house. Then I decided to do some weeding, and after that I tried to repair the back fence. I'm not very mechanical, but I straightened the fence a little. Then I walked around the yard again, remembering the day Mrs. Woodfin had given me a "tour" of it and loaned me a book on Blake. I had a lot of books to return to her, because over the past few months she had loaned me practically half her library. And they weren't all classics either. She had loaned me things like *The Sea Around Us* by Rachel Carson, and *Till We Have Faces* by C. S. Lewis, and *The Spire* by William Golding. I guess I had liked *The Spire* best, because even though it is very far-out and mystical it really moves you.

After a while I headed home, feeling tired and happy and thinking how great it was that school was out. Then I started thinking about the Peace rose and wondering how it had got its name—and that made me think about the draft. I had been thinking about the draft a lot lately, because it had finally dawned on me that it was going to happen to *me*. The draft had always been something that happened to other people, but now I realized that in four years I would have to go, and that if the war in Vietnam wasn't over by then, I would be one of those guys you see on television crawling through the mud. I wasn't sure about this, but I didn't think I was going to be one of those kids who burn their draft cards and go to jail. On the other hand, I was completely against killing—and to make things worse, this particular war didn't make sense to me. It was just like Mrs. Woodfin said: here was this little country divided in half and you were supposed to love one half of it and kill the other. They were all the same people, but you were supposed to protect half of them and mutilate the rest. Every time you turn on the radio they announce how many Vietcong we have killed—as though this were the solution to Communism. But it seemed to me that if we kept on killing them, there would be nobody left in that country at all. Which would really be a joke. We would win the war and rush in to make everybody democratic, and there wouldn't be anyone there.

One of the reasons my mother was so hot on college was because it would delay my being drafted. I had agreed with her about this once in a moment of weakness, but then it had occurred to me that it wasn't fair for all the dumb guys to get killed while the smart ones cooled their heels in college—drinking beer and dating and having a ball. Don't get me wrong. I'm not a hippie, but I do agree with them about war, because it seems very wrong to me that a lot of elderly world leaders should make wars and then expect kids to go and fight them. I just can't stand the idea of these elderly leaders sitting safe at their desks while millions of kids stumble around getting killed. Peter had written a poem about this very thing once, and Mrs.

Woodfin had quoted it to me. Part of it went like this:

No mockeries for them from prayers or bells,
Nor any voice of mourning save the choirs,
The shrill, demented choirs of wailing shells,
And bugles calling for them from sad shires.

It was too bad that Mrs. Woodfin didn't have Peter's book of poems, because I would have liked reading it. But the only copy she owned had been lost in a fire twenty years ago. *Bright Banners* was the title, and lately I had been wondering if I couldn't find it in one of those secondhand book stores in New York.

Oh well, I thought, I'll think about it tomorrow. Which is something a character named Scarlett O'Hara is always saying in a movie called *Gone With The Wind*. My mother took me to see a revival of it on my birthday, and it was the best movie I ever saw. Very old-fashioned, but colorful.

It had gotten late, and by the time I got home my father's car was in the driveway. I hurried up the steps and as I opened the front door I could smell this great smell of roast beef cooking. Orson was rolling around in the hall, playing with a catnip mouse. "Hi!" I called. "I'm home."

I went into the living room and my mother and father were sitting on the couch. They looked very grim, and I could see that they were angry because I was late again. Lateness is one of my worst problems.

"Listen," I said. "I'm sorry I took so long, but I had to plant that rosebush."

They were looking so strange that I couldn't figure out what was wrong. My father hadn't even made his first martini.

"Is anything wrong?" I asked.

My mother got up from the couch and walked over to the window and stood there. The sun was setting and everything looked very golden.

"She died," said my father after a few seconds. "Your friend."

At first I thought I hadn't heard him right. "What?"

"She had another heart attack."

"Mrs. Woodfin?"

"Yes."

"But Mrs. Woodfin is coming home in two days," I said.

"Albert," said my father, "the hospital just called. She died at three this afternoon."

23

I stood there for a minute—trying to understand what he was saying. I heard his words, but it was like I couldn't get the meaning. He was saying things I couldn't understand.

"The ladies in the ward were having a little party. It was somebody's birthday, and they wanted Mrs. Woodfin to recite for them. So she got out of bed and started to recite, and I guess she overtaxed herself or something, because …"

"I saw her this morning," I said. "I just fixed up her garden."

"Albert, she's dead."

"But Daddy …"

My mother came over and tried to touch me, but I pulled away from her.

"She's dead, son," said my father. "You'll have to accept it."

"And there are a few more things he'll have to accept," said my mother. She sounded very tense.

My father gave her a warning look. "Not now."

"Yes, now. Nothing can be achieved by …"

"Be quiet, Helen. He cared for that old lady."

"That's the point. Why can't he care about his family sometimes? He won't even let me touch him."

"That doesn't matter right now."

"It does matter! He only comes here to eat and sleep. You'd think it was a hotel. He can care about perfect strangers, but not his own family. Albert, the person who called from the hospital was a social worker. It seems that your friend Mrs. Woodfin was on welfare."

My father grabbed her arm. "For God's sake!"

"He's going to hear the truth! The person who called was named Miss Riley, and she knew Mrs. Woodfin very well because she was her caseworker. Mrs. Woodfin was never an actress, Albert. She was an old lady who used to teach English at a private school in New York. She was never on the stage, and she never had those fancy relatives you told us about."

These words were coming at me but I couldn't understand them. It was like I was a ghost.

"Mrs. Woodfin came from a very poor family in London, and she had been telling those lies for years. I guess she wanted to impress people, but none of the things she told you were true. She was just a spinster who came over to teach at the Crowley School in 1938, and who got fired for drinking. She worked in a bookstore and got fired for the same reason. An American relative left her the house down the block, and she went to live there on welfare because she was unemployable. She spent all of her money on liquor and couldn't pay her bills, and she told those stories to anyone who would listen. Why, Miss Riley said ..."

"Dammit!" my father shouted. "That's enough. How much do you think he can take? He's a child, Helen, a little boy. A year ago he was in grammar school. What do you want from him?"

"I want him to grow up!" said my mother.

"And be like you? Is that what you want?"

"Yes, that's exactly what I want."

"Well, you're not going to get away with it. He's my son,

too, and you've nagged him until he doesn't know who he is anymore. You're always trying to make him face the *truth*. What's so important about the truth? Why can't you just leave him alone?"

My father walked over and put his arms around me. "Albert," he said. "I'm so sorry."

And you know, it's funny, but for years I had wanted my father to do something like that. To put his arms around me or kiss me. I guess I had wanted that all my life. And now that he was doing it, I couldn't feel anything.

My mother lit a cigarette. "Let's have dinner. We'll all feel better after some dinner."

"Listen," I said. "I don't think I'll have any dinner right now. I think I'll just take a walk. I'm OK, really, but I'd like to take a walk."

"Do you want me to come with you?" asked my father. His arms were still around me.

"No, Daddy. I'm OK."

My mother called after me, but I didn't go back. I got my jacket and walked out to the street. Then I just stood there, because I didn't know where to go.

24

The sun had gone down, and the sky was purple. Street lights were coming on, and there was no one around. I started to walk towards the shopping center, and when I looked back I saw that Orson was following me.

I walked down through the development and crossed route 309. Then I came to the A&P, but I still kept on walking. Past Western Auto and the dry cleaners. Past the Dairy Queen. People were turning out the lights in their stores, and it was very quiet. I didn't know where I was going. I was just walking. And when I looked back the second time, Orson was gone.

Mrs. Woodfin, I thought, they say that you're dead, but I can't believe that. If I went to your house this minute, you would open the door and give me a cup of tea. And then we'd talk at the kitchen table. So I can't believe that you're dead. When my grandfather died, I could believe it, because there was no more reason for him to live. He was old and sick and confused. But you were different, and I can't believe that you're dead ...

After a while I came to a vacant lot near the Esso station. I guess I had been heading for it all along, because it was the one empty lot left in our town. They hadn't put a development or a factory on it yet. It was just a big lot filled with grass, and when you stood there you could see a mountain.

I walked through this lot for a few minutes, kicking at some stones, and then I started to cry.

I cried for a long time, and when I finished I knew that Mrs. Woodfin was dead and that nothing would bring her back. I hadn't even said good-bye to her. And she would never see the rosebush. They would just bury her somewhere, without her books or her velvet dress or any of the things she liked, and one day it would be as though she never lived. People die and you try to remember them, but you can't. They fade away, and eventually you can't even remember how they looked.

I thought about all the lies Mrs. Woodfin had told me, and I started crying again because I couldn't imagine why she had done it. I had been her friend, so why had she made up those stories about Peter and Bertie and Sarah Bernhardt? She didn't have to impress me. I was her friend, and I had never lied to her once. Then, though I didn't want to, I looked at her life and saw it the way it really was. I didn't want to do this, but I couldn't help it. I saw why she never had any food in the house or had the garbage picked up, and why the lights were always going out. I remembered her bottles of sherry and how she didn't have any visitors, and I realized that what my mother had said was true. She hadn't been anyone at all. Just an old lady who couldn't pay her bills. She had probably told her stories to so many people that I was the only one left to listen. And then this terrible anger came up in me like I was going to be sick, because I saw that Mrs. Woodfin had been like everybody else. An ordinary person, with nothing special in her life. I had loved her because she was special, and she was nobody. Just an alcoholic who told lies.

I had loved her.

I walked to the end of the lot and back again, kicking at stones and wanting to do something cruel. Something to hurt someone. There was a pain inside me, and I felt that it would never go away. Because for the rest of my life I would know that somebody I loved had tricked me. Maybe love doesn't hurt older people because they're used to it, But when a kid feels it for the first time, it's terrible, and you almost wish it hadn't happened because you don't know how to handle it. You wait all your life to love someone, and then you can't handle it at all.

I sat down on the grass and tried to stop crying. It was almost dark, with just a few streaks of purple left and one star. It was very quiet, and the cars on the highway sounded far away. I remembered what Mrs. Woodfin had said about owning the evening star. Then—like an ocean pouring down on me—I remembered everything she had ever said. I remembered how she had told me to be myself, and how she had said that the best people in the world were different. Shakespeare, Beethoven, St. Francis, Edison. I remembered that quotation about the drummer, and I remembered all the times she had made me feel good. How she had complimented me and told me that I should have dreams. I thought of New Zealand and the tugboats and Rilke and Blake and the books she had loaned me, and then, suddenly, as though my mind were racing too fast for me to catch up with it, I saw that Mrs. Woodfin *had* been special. It didn't matter that she had lied about herself because she was a lonely old woman who needed friends. What mattered was that she had made *me* feel different—and because of that, I had seen myself as a person for the first time in my life. Somebody called Albert Scully, who could be the biggest freak in the universe, but who would still be somebody. Mrs. Woodfin's life had been sad, and yet she had made poetry out of it with people like Peter and Bertie. She had believed the right things about what was good and beautiful—and so I had believed them, too. That was the point, the whole point, and it made Mrs. Woodfin special. Because she had given this thing to me ...

After a while I got up and zipped my jacket. I was tired, and my legs ached. I started to walk home, and as I walked I watched that star. It disappeared behind the gas station and then came out again, very bright. I thought of how my father had put his arms around me, and then I thought about the future. It would take me a long time to get over Mrs. Woodfin dying. I knew that. And when you came right down to it, my plans about New Zealand and the tugboats were far away. Because I would have to finish high school first. It was even possible that I would never get to New Zealand, and maybe nothing exciting would ever happen to me. I don't know. It was hard to say what would happen. And yet, in spite of everything, it was like Mrs. Woodfin said. I was going to be all right.